The House on Hanging Hill Lane

Book design by Vanessa Delbo Baker

Cover illustration by Mino
Author photograph by Tom Turner

The House on Hanging Hill Lane

Philip Alexander Baker

ACKNOWLEDGMENTS

This book could not have turned out how it did without the help, support and input from the following people who I will be grateful forever to.

My beta readers and story-loving friends who helped from the first idea to the last words: Tom Turner and Tom Menary for the story discussions and editors Kathy Towns and Tracey Govender for the story and line edits.

My filmmaking friends who include the above names, plus Tim and Kim Thorne from Sunsetrider Productions, Amanda and Neil Rowe from Rendered Pictures, Stan and Minna, Ash and Alex, Candice and Martin. Paramore Productions. And everyone else. Detective Amanda for her help with Cornish police protocol. Mother Horror, Sadie Hartmann, for making me get up and do this, whether she knew it or not.

Everyone who helped with the video for this book: Ben, John and Sam, Kim and Tim, Candice, Kathy, Helen and Colin, Fletch and Laura, Rich, Sarah, Stuart Partridge, and especially Amanda and Neil Rowe.

And, of course, my family: Mum and Dad, who showed me what a book should look like. Sarah for all the help. Louise and James. And most of all, my wonderful book designer and even more wonderful wife, Vanessa.

Prologue

First it killed the five who lived at ten,
The four at eight were next to die, and then...

The three at six were nailed to their door,
Then darkness came to take the two at four...

So now it falls to me to bring to you,

The story of the single girl,
Alone, at number
Two.

CHAPTER ONE

Daphne's face was hiding again.

A thick, teary mess of eye shadow and mascara obscured most of her skin and a heavy tangle of black hair hung over her eyes, right down her face and past her chin. The perfect hiding place.

How had it come to this? She'd desperately loved her mother, and now she was gone. You can't blame anyone for crying like that, least of all a lost eighteen-year-old who'd never known her father, now motherless for reasons that just didn't make sense.

There's nothing you can do or say at a time like this, but that didn't stop Olivia from trying. Daphne's beautifully dressed best friend in the colourful clothes was holding a three-pronged black steel candlestick, the last of the packing, which she dropped gently into the box as Daphne peered through a gap in her hair.

'She was a cool lady,' said Olivia, a little older and wiser than Daphne, parting her friend's wet hair with her fingers to see the girl behind the mess. 'She was as mad as you, with her silly hats and magical smile.' Olivia glanced around the room. 'Is that everything?'

'Do you have my scissors?' Daphne had been a clothes maker and a student of fashion, though she'd been seriously thinking about dropping out for a while now. She now had not just an excuse but a genuine reason, and it was time to go home. She still wanted her special scissors, of course. A gift from her mother long ago, those scissors had cut a lot of fabric, yet still nothing cut quite like them. Aside from the sharp pain she was feeling at that moment, perhaps. Olivia pulled them out of a drawer and passed them over.

'Come on then. Let's get you home.'

A house is an impossible dream for many a teenager, but a nightmare when you've received it as a result of your only parent dying. She wouldn't be able to sell it either, even if she'd known where to start. Houses on Hanging Hill Lane were always hard to sell. Its old houses, many on the verge of disrepair, seemed to somehow match its creepy past. Most of the families had been on that street for generations. Now one old house was falling to Daphne, an artist in secret and shy college drop-out, too young to want any of the responsibilities that come with an old house. Houses in England can be old, often well over a hundred years. These houses were much older still. Number two leaked and whistled in the wind and the pipes made a creaky racket when the hot water ran through.

'I'm scared,' was all Daphne could muster before the tears started again. 'I don't want it. I don't want to go back there. It's so cold and full of memories.'

Olivia smiled warmly as she always did.

'Stay here then. It's not too late.' She didn't really mean it and they both knew it. Though Olivia could persuade almost anyone to do anything, these weren't words of persuasion, but words of comfort. They half worked. Daphne pulled the key off her keyring and held it out to her friend.

'I'll visit. I'll be round all the time.'

'Keep it,' replied Olivia, closing Daphne's fingers around the key and holding her hand tightly. 'Ready?'

***

There's something quite beautiful about two young adults in an open-topped car driving through the British countryside. If nothing else, there are only a few days in the year sunny enough for that, and it's the ultimate sign that summer might have finally arrived. If only the mood inside the car had matched the happy picture it made – not helped by a large box labelled 'art stuff' crammed uncomfortably onto Daphne's lap with the corner digging painfully into her thigh. These small cars aren't ideal for moving house, and the backseat was bouncing busily with boxes and three half-dressed mannequins, looking lively as they bobbed and jumped around with the cracked and warty surface of the old country road.

Olivia wasn't built for moods like this, so reached for the one escape into possible better times: the stereo. There are some songs that can just lift moods, and this was one of them. Olivia, cautiously and with half an eye on her friend, started to sing along with a perfectly magical voice. No bad reaction from Daphne, so she started to ramp it up just a little, singing a little louder, and throwing over a quick smile to her friend, half buried under the box which rattled over every little bump.

Daphne loved that about Olivia. If the music hadn't gone down well, she'd have changed it for sure. Olivia really saw Daphne, and she was hugely grateful for that. With almost everyone else, she just felt invisible, as is often the case for shy young women little over five feet tall. No one saw her and she never felt like she'd fitted in at college. But Olivia saw everything.

The car passed a herd of ponies in the fields, the colts now young adults after the spring, and that was enough to raise the corners of Daphne's mouth just a little bit – and Olivia wasn't going to miss that opportunity. Up went the volume. Up went the energy. Up went Olivia's infectious smile, tanned by the years of growing up by the sea, and Daphne couldn't help but follow.

By the time they reached Hanging Hill Lane, they were both grinning like children, the car slowing down and navigating large old potholes and a steep, winding descent. But who was that on the roadside, watching? The lady, around sixty years old or a little older, stood completely motionless with a stock-still stare right into Daphne's being.

'Not sure about the neighbours, Daph,' said Olivia. 'She looks weird.'

'That's Deanna Tamblyn. She's lived here forever. My mum used to bicker with her outside after I'd gone to bed, but I never really met her,' replied Daphne, as she watched Deanna disappear out of sight in her wing mirror. Deanna stared back the whole time, never moving a muscle but to slowly twist her neck to watch the car disappear down the winding, leafy hill.

The car pulled up at the final house, right next to the road sign. Hanging Hill Lane. The end of the road itself had almost been reclaimed by the neighbouring woodland down at that far end, and there was no clear distinction where the concrete might have ended and the woods began. It was the place where the civilised human part of the world stopped and the natural world began. The place where you could step between the two worlds.

A place where five large rocks sat in a high pile and had done since as long as any human alive could remember.

'Here we are then,' smiled Olivia gently. 'Number two,' not realising they were being watched.

On the opposite side of the road stood a red-haired lady in her late fifties, sweeping her driveway with an old-styled straw broom, staring straight at the girls with no expression at all on her face. The pair, focused on the house and each carrying a heavy box, didn't even notice, until they returned for the mannequins.

The red-haired lady watched first the girls and then the door of number two long after it was closed, still as a statue, aside from gently sweeping the leafy ground. She was still standing there watching as the sun dipped down

6

over the house and Olivia was leaving for the night. Olivia's half-smile wasn't returned by the red-haired lady as she got in and started the engine. 'Weird bitch,' she muttered to herself as she drove back up the steep winding hill, middle finger stuck up to the grey Deanna Tamblyn, still standing at the top, motionless in the moonlight, neck twisting back as her firm gaze watched Olivia's car disappear out of sight.

CHAPTER TWO

There's always that weird and uncomfortable feeling inside any house owned by someone who's just died. But this house wasn't now owned by the recently deceased, but by Daphne, who'd rushed straight back before the horrible news of her mother's passing had even started to sink in. 'If anything should happen to me,' her mother had always said, 'you get straight back here, okay? You're needed.' She'd said it often, and Daphne had always promised. It had happened so often and from such a young age that she never thought it was strange, just like all the other weird things we're taught are normal as kids and so grow up still believing until we die. But it still felt odd in that old, cold house. Uncomfortable. It still felt like her mum's place.

But now, there was no mother. Just Daphne with three mannequins for company, placed side by side in the lounge, and a load of boxes being slowly unpacked or stashed away in the dusty old storeroom opposite the lounge for when the sight of the contents might hurt a little less. A box labelled 'Mum' remained strapped shut for exactly that reason, and if she was to be like anyone else in the world, it could stay that way for the next thirty years or more. No one wants to open a box of hurt like that. Still, that one didn't go into the store room. That one stayed in the lounge. She wasn't ready to hide her mother away quite yet.

A slightly less painful box was labelled 'kitchen,' and Daphne struggled with it well enough to get it onto the countertop without breaking too much inside. What a fascinating kitchen it was. A black, well-used steel whistling kettle lived on the old stovetop alongside a giant dented cooking pot which sparked many childhood memories. Knives, rather than hiding in a drawer, hung ready on a rack a little over head height. A taller person in the dark might have drawn blood on those blades, if not alert to the ever-hanging danger. Like the scissors, it seemed after all these decades, they never blunted.

Then there was the beautifully elaborate oak-carved herb rack, and the huge cast iron oven which could get burning hot in minutes, with massive flames that visibly danced as they burned brightly behind the smoke-stained glass. Once, years ago and for reasons she was too young to remember, she'd seen a whole pig's head cooking in there, and the image had stuck with her over the years. As she cooked, every last one of these things sparked memories of her eccentric but kind mother. She'd never found herbs that smelled like that anywhere else she'd ever been in her whole life. It would've been beautifully nostalgic if not for the pain that elbowed its way to the front to block the beauty.

The herbs would have made for a delicious stew too if it weren't for the accompanying emotional pain that completely ruined her appetite. As she sat down on the old lounge sofa, with tears and immense sadness returning to cut through her tiredness, she was only temporarily distracted from her thoughts when a twirling blue light danced through the front window which overlooked the road. She closed the curtains, left her half-eaten food in the bowl on the floor like she did when she was a kid, and went to bed. And, eventually, to sleep.

Sleep. Nothing but darkness and stillness.

It was almost like peace.

***

As morning came, quietness left, first with the alarm clock and then the doorbell, something her mother had only recently installed after the same huge brass door-knocker had banged on the door for well over a hundred years. The old knocker remained, and the slightly incongruous-looking button was the first sign to Daphne that this wasn't the same house she'd grown up in.

Daphne checked through the glass spyhole, another recent addition, to see a familiar and very friendly face she hadn't seen for a long time, and another, smaller face that hadn't even existed the last time the two has seen each other. Opening the thick wooden door, Daphne let out a huge smile to Sara, her next-door neighbour she'd grown up with, and in Sara's arms, Alfie, a very young baby with an unbelievably sweet face.

'Hello beautiful, I didn't know you were out of the hospital yet,' said Daphne to her childhood friend, now in her early twenties. 'And hello you, beautiful tiny human. Welcome to our world.'

As Sara entered, so did the closest thing to a feeling of belonging that Daphne had felt for a while. She hadn't realised she'd missed that feeling until right then when it came back. Sara was living alone as a single mother, and Daphne knew that Alfie, so tiny, was going to become a big part of her life.

The old whistling kettle made a fantastic sound as it boiled, flooding Daphne with memories once more. The tea tasted good with extra sugar, just how her mother had always made it. Sitting with a warm, sweet cup of tea with Sara was the first time she'd felt almost comfortable in this house since it had become hers.

'Wait, I've got something for you,' said Daphne as she pulled something from a half-unpacked box, and passed it over to Sara who looked utterly delighted. The cow-shaped, baby-sized onesie looked a perfect fit for little Alfie, if certainly not perfectly made. Alfie grabbed it and squeezed. Sara looked over the moon.

'Alfie's my first customer, and he's the cutest baby in the world!' said Daphne, just as Alfie vomited on himself and his gift. It was the perfectly wrong time for the doorbell to ring.

As Sara took Alfie to the bathroom for a clean, Daphne answered the door to two police officers, one in a black suit holding an ID badge, and the other in uniform, looking at the floor nervously.

'I'm sorry to interrupt your day,' said the man with the badge. Daphne caught the name, DS Hart, just before he dropped it and let it swing on his lanyard. 'We're conducting a door-to-door after an incident on this street. Do you have a few minutes?'

'Incident?' replied Daphne.

'A serious one, I'm afraid. Could we come in?'

Sara and Alfie arrived back into the lounge just as the officers sat down, a little shocked to see the police uniform.

'You are, please?' asked DS Hart.

'Sara Hunter, I live next door.'

'Ah, well we've found you then, please sit down.'

Sara perched herself on the edge of the sofa next to Daphne, clutching Alfie, now visibly tiring. The other officer could barely make eye contact, and gripped his pad firmly, ready to make notes.

'I was in the hospital,' said Sara, explaining her absence and wondering why they'd been looking for her.

'Have you noticed anything suspicious around here recently? Particularly over the last few days?' said Hart, not taking his eyes off Sara. The girls shook their heads. 'How well did you know the Stephensons at number ten?'

'They were the new family,' said Sara. 'The first new family here for years. Since I've been alive, I think.'

'I've never met them,' said Daphne, softly.

'Unfortunately, and we'd like to ask you to keep this to yourselves for the time being, they were found dead in their home this morning. We don't mean to alarm you, but we do need to ask for any possible witnesses. Early information can be vital.' Sara clutched Alfie tighter, who let out a small cry.

'I didn't see anything, that's horrible,' said Daphne, her feelings of grief for her mother making way for feelings of shock and fear.

'Don't worry, Sara, was it?' chimed in a suddenly confident PC Lamb to Sara. Even in the seriousness and shock of the situation, the sudden faked confidence jarred. 'We'll catch him. Don't you worry about a thing.' After a quick pause, he pretended to rub something off his shoe that wasn't ever there, and looked back down at his notebook. Daphne turned her mind back to what was going on.

'All of them? How many were there?'

'We can't give out all the details right no—' Hart was interrupted by Sara.

'Five. A couple and three kids. They seemed so lovely. The Dad always made a joke about Deanna Tamblyn standing around near his house.' Alfie cried a little more.

'So you haven't been around for a few days or seen anything at all? Nothing?' he said to Sara. The girls shook their heads with such similarity that they could have been sisters, Daphne starting to wonder what she had to do to not be invisible, even in her own home. It was a familiar feeling.

'If you hear anything, give us a call.' He passed Sara a card with his details and started to stand. PC Lamb suddenly clapped his hands loudly and stood quickly, making the girls jump a little and Alfie cry harder.

'Stay safe, Sara, we've got you covered anyway.'

The police left the girls sitting on the sofa and the front door thudded shut.

'I'm gonna go home, ring mum and sort this one out,' said Sara, standing with Alfie. 'Give me a text later if you want me to come round. Not too late though, you know,' she said glancing at her newborn with a worried smile. 'Thanks for the onesie, it's beautiful.' Sara turned to leave with a compassionate half-smile, the best she could manage. The front door thudded shut again as Daphne sank back in her chair.

'Jesus,' she said out loud, and reached for her comforting cup of tea.

CHAPTER THREE

With her hair still wet and wrapped in a towel from her morning shower, Daphne was just three stairs up on her way to her room, noticing the distinct, familiar and now nostalgic creak the second step had made for as long as she could remember. The old wooden steps were carpeted now, but the wood still creaked loudly underneath, and always with exactly the same sound. Her climb was interrupted by the doorbell, still an unfamiliar noise that didn't quite match this old house. She grabbed her dressing gown from her childhood bedroom and step two creaked again as she walked back down towards the door.

Through the spyhole, she could see two smartly suited men, one tall with attractive black hair but as thin as a beansprout, the other short with a suit that fitted his fat body so badly she could tell even through the spyhole. She opened the door, awkwardly half-hiding her robe-dressed body behind the door.

'Hello?'

'Good morning,' said the beansprout in the immaculate suit. His west-coast American accent stood out straight away. You don't get that many non-local folk out in the sticks in deepest Cornwall, let alone people from as far away as the USA. 'My name is Timothy. I was wondering if I could take a moment to talk to you about our Saviour?'

Great, thought Daphne. *It's the God-Squad.* Daphne hadn't been brought up religious in any way, though her mother had always told her not to lose an open mind about any and all possibilities. But pushy Christians were never welcome on Hanging Hill Lane, and Daphne remembered once as a young child watching a pair of Jehovah's Witnesses getting comedically shooed away up the steep hill by Deanna Tamblyn with an old straw broom.

'I'm sorry,' Daphne replied politely, slightly frustrated that she'd answered the door when it would have been better to ignore it. 'This is a bad time.'

The short man hadn't blinked once, slightly creeping out the naked-feeling teenager.

'We won't be a minute, and this is urgent,' the short man said in a local accent, frustrating Daphne. His eyes were darting where they weren't welcome to dart, too.

'Would it be better if we came back later?' interjected beansprout Timothy, putting Daphne a little more at ease. He was a mildly charismatic man despite his googly eyes, and Daphne couldn't help but notice, though she was very aware that if she stuck around for a conversation it would have been most definitely awkward. She was an introvert at heart and uncomfortable with strangers, particularly pushy ones who wanted to talk about a God she had no interest in.

'Later would be better,' she answered, pushing the door closed. Timothy had barely got out his next question, something about what time would be best perhaps, when the door was firmly shut. A conversation about Jesus was the last thing she felt like. She was cold and wanted to get dressed and the cold morning breeze from outside just made it worse. Sometimes, she wished she could just make herself invisible and be done with it.

Minutes later and much more comfortable in her snug woolly jumper, Daphne sat calmly in her lounge sewing. Her fingers barely moved and the stitching was wonky. She was just going through the motions now, clinging on to the last of a dream she no longer really had. She occasionally glanced down from the television but didn't care. This wasn't her anymore. And then the needle stopped. The news reporter with the long black hair had said something that took all of Daphne's attention and filled her stomach with a dark, heavy dread.

'More breaking news on the unexplained deaths that have shocked the community and the country as a whole. Details have been released that the police have now opened a murder enquiry, with unconfirmed reports that all five members of the family died from trauma to the head. The family, the youngest of which was just twelve years old we understand, have been identified and police are still appealing for witnesses and for information that might be of assistance. Next of kin have been informed and we hope to bring you more on the story as we get it. This is Angela Shipman for CMT News.'

Daphne felt sick. She'd not met the new family at number ten but it was only four houses from her up the hill, right on the street where she grew up. She'd walked past that house every single day on the way to school. Every single walk on the way to the post office or village shop. Every time she went anywhere at all, aside from a walk in Hanging Hill Woods at the bottom of the hill, she'd walked right past that house. Now something utterly terrible had happened there, just as she'd moved back to the road, alone and already suffering. Her stomach turned with disgust churned up with fear. But more, she suddenly felt very alone. Every creak in that quiet old house seemed to become crystal clear and close. The safety she'd felt there as a child was gone, replaced by the feeling of a looming threat every time something outside scratched or an old pipe groaned. She was alone, and she knew it. That was, until the doorbell rang once more. *Who now?* she thought, picking up the TV remote and switching it off.

She must've been seeing things. Just for that split second as the ancient tube TV went from on to off, a face had flashed up on the screen. Or had it? Surely not? Just her mind playing tricks, perhaps. Or just a random pattern in the cathode tube-produced dots that had looked just a little like a face, and her stressed mind had filled in the gaps. But that doesn't mean it wasn't creepy as Hell. Daphne didn't like that one bit, and crossed her arms in front of her and shuddered, trying to shake off the creepy shivers.

The recently-installed spyhole was already getting a lot of use. Timothy waited again, as did his companion with the permanently open wandering eyes. She had no intention of answering, but stayed to watch until they left. The pair waited and tried the doorbell again. Daphne kept her eye to the hole the whole time, breathing as quietly as possible. Eventually the men gave up and stepped back, turned, and left, revealing a figure across the road. Initially concealed by Timothy but now clearly visible, was the red-haired lady, standing completely still, watching back. It felt like she was looking straight through the door and into her eyes, though she couldn't have been. Daphne held on a little longer to see what the red-haired lady was doing. The answer was nothing. Nothing but staring back. It made no sense. Perhaps, like Deanna, she had something against the religious door-knocking folk, and was watching them. But it didn't feel that way. And then another figure approached the red-haired lady. A face she could only just make out but was very familiar. It was Gugwana, the only non-white lady in the whole village when Daphne was growing up, and she hadn't aged a day. She still wore the same beautiful, long and colourful clothes that had made Daphne consider training in fashion in the first place.

As Gugwana reached the red-haired lady, she stopped and turned to face Daphne's door too. A smile and a wave right at Daphne were too much and she retreated quickly from the spyhole. Gugwana was always lovely, but that? That was just plain weird.

***

Things felt like they were getting too much. Of course they were. No eighteen-year-old should have to deal with what poor Daphne was going through, and now there was a real possibility she was seeing things. So she turned to the one thing she always turned to in times of high stress: painting.

Her easel was set up in her bedroom, surrounded by paint pots and brushes and holding a large canvas. Daphne's art technique started with a sharp pencil outline, though she often moved to a paintbrush before the outline was finished, and she always started off by sharpening the pencil with a knife. There were pencil shavings on the floor beneath the easel from years of painting since she was a young girl. She never cleaned them up and saw them as memories, a growing show of all her work at the easel that she didn't want to remove, as if getting rid of them would somehow also erase some of her past. Next came big brush strokes. Then, she'd put all that away and with her tiny brush and little pots, she'd fill the details with splashes and dots. It was a unique style of art and she'd likely have sold one or two paintings if only she'd believed in her work a bit more. But creating art for strangers wasn't why she did it. It was her way to get lost in something, take her mind away from what the world claimed to be reality, and finally forget the stresses in her life. Today, she needed to paint more than ever and dropped the pencil with the canvas still almost completely blank.

Seconds after the brush stroked the canvas for the first time, she was gone. Thinking about her mother's magical smile, not realising she was giving a little subconscious smile back that had magic in it too. Thinking about her recent times living with Olivia and what a lovely person she was and how lucky she'd been to find a college housemate like her. Thinking about fond childhood times with her mother and Sara. Finally, for the first time in days, she started to relax.

Being in her childhood home was bringing back memories. She remembered being out in the back garden picking up a variety of bugs at just four years old, and putting them in her mother's giant cooking pot that was old and dented even back then. She even found a newt once and dropped that in. Probably from the small pond in the nearby woods, she guessed, where she used to go and look at the toads and occasionally see a hare run by, and hide and stare at the old homeless woman who would wash her clothes in the stream under the bridge. She didn't know why she'd collected bugs, it was just a hobby she'd developed on her own. Perhaps as an only child these tiny beings were the only company she had when her mother was busy and Sara wasn't allowed to come and play. It's where she'd started to rhyme, too. *Beetle* rhymed with *people*. *Spider* with *fighter*. She'd loved rhymes as a kid. *Hug* and *bug*. Her mother had never seemed to mind the bugs in the cooking equipment, and even seemed somehow quite proud. None of the little creatures ever got hurt, though. Her mother would always release them. So she said, anyway.

Bees and *cheese*. She'd always liked that one.

Daphne had known what she loved back then, even if it was just gathering critters in a large pot and rhyming them. As her hand painted with precision, her mind wandered in some kind of half meditation. Why had she stayed at college for almost two years when she'd hated it after a few days? She knew fashion wasn't for her. It was Olivia, wasn't it? Such a wonderful and encouraging person. At twenty-two, Daphne thought she was old for a potential friend when they'd met, but really started to look up to her. That encouragement had worked wonders and kept Daphne going. But now, away from it all and deep in a state of flow, she realised she'd have been better off without. She'd wasted all those months because of a lovely girl being so supportive and encouraging. It wasn't Olivia's fault. She'd been a perfect friend. But now Daphne just didn't know what she wanted, or even who she particularly was, and had no mother to go to anymore. No one to help work things out. Even if she'd still been alive, she'd have only been cryptic about it. *Let Daphne grow into herself*, was always her philosophy. *Let her make mistakes. Just be gentle with her.* Now there was no one to guide her, even if the guidance she'd always had didn't seem to make any sense. It wasn't like she could just go back to bugs and rhymes, either. *Magic* and *tragic*. That was a new one. She liked the bug ones better.

As the stress subsided, the strange things she'd seen seemed to make more sense. That face on the TV? That was just random dots plus stress. She'd watched plenty of psychology videos on the internet and knew all about the concept of patternicity, where humans see shapes where they aren't there and join dots where there's no actual connection, like seeing monsters in the clouds. Maybe she'd seen it happen to a character in an old horror film, too. She wasn't sure. Patternicity, a film scene memory plus the anxiety from the news of the murders would explain that very easily. And Gugwana? Probably waving at someone else, just out of sight. Those spyholes bend reality and make the distance look so small and unclear. If anything, it was actually lovely to see her, and under normal circumstances she'd have opened the door and said hello if she wasn't feeling too shy. But it all seemed a bit weird under the stress and she was feeling even more anxious than normal. At least things were starting to make a little sense now. Patternicity. Stress. An unclear spyhole. Who was the red-haired lady though? Daphne had memories of a lady with red hair in the house across the road, looking out the window into the woodland through the net curtain, but she was known as a hermit and Daphne didn't recall seeing her outside once. No one else new had moved into the street for years, Sara had said to the policeman, so maybe that was her. Maybe she'd conquered her shyness and stepped outside. Or maybe not. Memories look hazy through a lens of anxiety.

And yet other things were crystal clear. Her memory of shouting at the school bully at thirteen years old to get off the small boy still plagued her. No one seemed to hear or care, and the pain she felt of being invisible was probably almost as bad as the pain being felt by the poor small boy, whose name she couldn't remember. She'd felt so inadequate and sad after that. Then there were the night terrors that had pinned her to her bed in the dark of night, until her mother would rush in to calm her. Those terrifying visions had stayed in her memory as clear as the nights they had come to fill her with dread and cover her with sweat, embedding their trauma so deeply into her neural pathways that they'd leave the remnants of fear with her for days and often weeks. There was always a little bit that never left. They had mounted up and joined forces and still lived inside her.

Her happier memories with Sara were as clear as day too. Daphne was still shy and still felt like she didn't really fit in at college, and blamed that on her being an only child. But she wasn't completely alone growing up. Sara would pop around and they'd get up to mischief, but because Sara was so much older she'd always pin the blame on Daphne, who wouldn't get into trouble because she was so young. It worked like magic. One time they'd started a fire in the back garden at Sara's place after hearing you could do it just by rubbing sticks together. They hadn't meant to cause such an inferno, or even expected it to work. But it had done, only too well, and young Daphne took the blame as always and got away with a speech about being careful with fire while Sara got away with it completely.

Then there was the time that they'd been out on the street chasing a wild hare and a van had almost hit Daphne. The sweating delivery driver claimed not to have seen her, and Sara had basically blackmailed him into not telling their parents by blaming him rather than the child jumping out into the road.

They'd grown up a lot since then, but the bond remained, even though they'd not seen each other for a while. But now she was back, alone, and already needed Sara more than ever. Tony. That was the name of the small boy. Or Tom. It was one or the other, she was sure. And what was that rumour the other children would talk about? Something strange on the street. That memory was hazy too. The anxiety lens was thicker on that one.

As the world fell into darkness, Daphne lay down her brushes and was on her back in bed, not exactly at peace but feeling a little better. Not even the house was creaking. As she dozed off to sleep, for the first time in far too long, it felt like nothing was happening.

Because in that dark, quiet house, nothing *was* happening.

Nothing but a stressed and grieving teenager, brand new to adulthood, sleeping.

Nothing but three mannequins standing still in the dark lounge.

Nothing but knives hanging on a rack with barely a swing from a slight breeze.

Nothing but a single drip falling from the tap.

Nothing. Until the alarm clock rang, and an even stranger day began.

CHAPTER FOUR

The toaster was new too. Her mother had always used the old gas grill, but it seemed like just recently she was upgrading and modernising a few things she didn't even care for, as if she was preparing to hand over the house to someone younger. The toast popped up with an unfamiliar sound just as another new sound that was now becoming a little too familiar ding-donged through the hallway. The spyhole revealed PC Lamb, waiting alone.

'Hello again, just a standard follow-up about number ten. I'm just checking if you've seen or heard anything since our chat, or if anything's come to mind?'

'No, nothing.'

'Nothing at all that doesn't feel right?'

Daphne shook her head, knowing the strange things she'd experienced weren't exactly a matter for the police. 'Sorry,' she said softly.

'Sorry to bother you then, I'll be off,' Lamb said professionally as he turned and walked back up the road. The countryside street looked unlike Daphne had ever seen it before. The leaves, normally so green at the height of summer, were already starting to die and fall. It was always so calm and quiet, and now there were police cars, serious-looking officials and even a few people being turned away trying to get a view or a snap of the now newsworthy street. A woman, possibly Angela Shipman from the TV news, was just visible on the bend. It looked like her from afar, anyway. But a smell of smoke had Daphne running back to the kitchen before she could confirm. When the smoke alarm went off she nearly jumped out of her skin. Her mother must have installed that recently too, and not said a word.

Smoke streamed from the toaster as she pressed the button to pop out the toast again, now burned to a crisp. Daphne switched off the alarm, pulled out her phone, and scrolled through her address book all the way to *S. S* for Sara, of course.

In the lounge, the two young women drank tea again, as the British do in such times of stress, or any other time one has a guest, for that matter. Alfie slept peacefully as the smell of smoke subsided.

'Do you know the red-haired lady from across the road?' asked Daphne.

'Of course, that's Morwenna at number one. Been there, like, forever.'

'Morwenna?'

'Morwenna Rowe. Mum always said she was very kind. Quiet though, total hermit, and maybe a little strange.'

Daphne laughed.

'She's definitely a little bit strange. She kind of gives me the creeps. And what's with those God-Squad door-knockers? The short one's the weirdest. Was everyone around here always odd or am I just noticing now because I've been away?' Daphne hadn't chatted so much or so confidently for a while.

'I haven't had any God-Squad for years, I think Deanna frightened them all away,' laughed Sara, just as the doorbell rang yet again.

'Speak of the Devil,' said Daphne, standing up and turning with a smile. 'See what I did there?'

Through the spyhole, standing a little too close, was Gugwana. Her skin looked just as shiny and beautiful as it always had done. She must be nearly seventy now, thought Daphne, but looked flawless. It was Daphne's chance to say hello to this old, friendly face who'd been so kind to her as a child, and regularly covered for this pair's mischief too. She opened the door with a huge, excited smile, partly there to mask her shyness which never really fully left, whoever she was with. Aside from Sara, of course.

But Gugwana didn't smile back. She looked deadly serious, right at her, scouring Daphne's face as if she was checking every single freckle and pore.

'Hi Gugwana,' Daphne said awkwardly, her smile dropping fast, but got no response at all. Nothing. Nothing but Gugwana's fingers on Daphne's cheek, inspecting her whole face deeply with serious eyes.

'Are you okay?' asked Daphne, now thinking things were getting far too strange. There was an uncomfortableness about the situation that didn't make sense. Gugwana had always been a kind lady with a special, distinctive smile that could light up the dark. A person who could put anyone at ease. But this was just a shell of the beautiful lady she remembered. Dementia, perhaps, and young Daphne didn't know how to deal with it – especially when Gugwana put two fingers into Daphne's left eye and pulled the eyelids wide apart, staring in for a deep look, the two women's widening pupils barely three inches apart.

'I have to go.' Daphne closed the door quickly with a familiar thud. There was so much that didn't feel right. Not just about Gugwana's strange behaviour, but by how badly she'd just treated an old family friend, so she fought her awkwardness and opened the door again. Gugwana was gone. She wasn't to be seen at all and must have moved very quickly. Perhaps the age hadn't got to her physically like it had her mind. Instead, a little way up the hill, a hare hopped across the road, reminding Daphne again of her childhood and the time she almost got hit by the delivery driver. Hares were common in the area with the woodland being so close, and she'd always enjoyed spotting them as a kid. Now, one provided a little moment of happiness in an otherwise horrible moment of strangeness.

Daphne returned to the lounge, a little confused and upset, and sat back down.

'Has everything been alright with Gugwana? I didn't know she was ill.'

'She's fine,' replied Sara.

'That was her. She seemed... weird.'

'Not everyone here is weird, Daphne. Trust me, she's fine.' Sara smiled into her mug and took another sip.

'You just said, what was her name, Morwenna? You said she's weird.'

'A bit.'

'And Deanna?' Daphne said with a knowing smile.

'Deanna grows on you. Anyway, why is it so cold in here? You're tiny Daphne, you'll freeze!' But Daphne's attention had been taken away from the conversation.

'What's that smell?' she asked.

'I better get him home,' replied Sara. 'This one needs changing.'

'Jesus Christ, Alfie,' said Daphne, trying not to laugh. 'You are evil!'

'I'll let myself out. Text me.' Sara got up and left quickly before the smell spread too fast. Looking out the front window ready to wave goodbye to Sara, Daphne saw a still figure across the road. It was red-haired Morwenna Rowe, staring in through the window. Seconds after the front door thudded shut, Sara walked back past the window clutching Alfie and gave a little laugh and a wave in as she walked by. Daphne's attention then turned back to Morwenna, but she was gone. She closed the curtains. No one wants strangers staring into their house, least of all a lone grieving teenage girl living just four doors down from the scene of a brutal murder. *Murder* rhymes with *observer*, she thought. *Yuck.*

***

The next time Daphne made a cup of tea, she called a good friend while waiting for the whistle of the kettle.

'Olivia!' she called out as she connected. The two hadn't spoken since they'd driven down together, and Olivia hadn't realised the murder in the news was on the road she'd been on just a couple of days before. They chatted for a while and Daphne felt a little happier, an effect Olivia had had on her countless times before. 'I don't know if I've done the right thing, Liv,' Daphne said, changing the mood to a more serious tone. 'Everything was great living with you. Things are a little weird back here.'

'Yeah I saw at least two weirdos in the thirty seconds I was on that road,' replied Olivia. An unnatural pause. 'Daphne? You there love?'

'Um, Olivia?' said Daphne, confused, staring out her kitchen window into the back garden.

'What?'

'There's someone in my garden. She's looking at me. This is weird as Hell.'

What was even more weird than someone being outside in her own back garden staring at her, was the fact that the intruder was sitting in a tree. She could just about tell it was a woman, but her face was obscured by a grey shawl and browning leaves. It was a horrible feeling, and one Daphne wanted to get rid of.

'I've got to go,' she said hanging up just as Olivia's tiny phone-voice had started to ask what was going on.

Daphne ran to the front door, knowing there was a good police presence around. PC Foot was six feet tall and well-built, if a little chubby, and looked noticeably nervous as he approached.

'Are you okay?' asked Foot, seeing Daphne's distress.

'There's someone in my garden staring at me.'

'Let's take a look,' said Foot, and radioed his colleagues to number two in case the situation got dangerous.

The view from the kitchen window revealed nothing.

Nothing but the empty tree gently swaying in the breeze. Nothing but the quiet garden where the critters were now safe from being put in a pot by a young Daphne. Nothing but the thin wooden fence that wouldn't protect anyone from anything. And certainly no woman in a tree.

'She was just there, sitting in that tree.'

'Yeah, that's a bit weird, do you want me to take a look in the garden?'

But the garden was well in view, and there wasn't much point. Whoever it was, assuming Daphne wasn't seeing things again, was long gone.

'There's nothing you can do is there?' asked Daphne.

'We'll go round the back and find whoever it was. We won't be taking any chances with the houses up the road like that. I'll get someone to come and ask some questions and I'll go and get on this for you.'

'Wait. Houses? Something else has happened?' asked Daphne as they walked to the front door and PC Foot stepped outside.

'I'm sorry, someone will be around to brief you soon and ask some questions. I need to go and get the back checked for you.' As he walked off he turned around briefly and spoke confident words but with a nervous face. 'Anything you need, just lean out the door and shout, we're always out here at the moment.'

'Thank you,' replied Daphne as she watched PC Foot accelerate off up the road speaking into his radio. She was just stepping back inside when she was surprised by two men right behind her.

'I'm glad we caught you,' said Timothy in his American accent that reminded her very quickly who he was.

Great, the beansprout God man.

'Sorry we missed you last night. You said you'd like to hear more about the Saviour.'

Daphne was still a good couple of yards from her doorway, out in the open with the two men and not at all in the mood to hear about Jesus, and retreated quickly towards her open door and the feeling of safety.

'I'm sorry, now isn't a good time,' she said, putting one hand on her door as she stepped in, readily but politely showing she wanted to close it in a way that shy people learn to do very well.

'It won't take long, just a few minutes of your time.'

But Daphne wasn't in the mood for this and started to close the door.

'I'm sorry,' she said, but the sight she saw in that second before the door closed was one that disturbed her greatly. The fat friend's face turned deadly serious and stared right between Daphne's eyes. But weirder still were the words that came from his clenched jaw.

'There is a war coming, Miss Locke.'

The door thudded shut and the lock clicked with Daphne safe inside, confused, scared, and desperately not wanting to be alone anymore. Something very worrying had just come out of that man's mouth. Not about the war. They were just the words of yet another weirdo. But *Miss Locke*? How and why would they know her name?

CHAPTER FIVE

The old whistling kettle was starting to become a familiar sound again, and the nostalgia of it was starting to wear away. Still, it was always comforting, either because it reminded her of the good old days or because some part of her brain had connected the whistle with the near-arrival of a sweet, hot cup of tea.

Daphne had no wish to spend the evening alone and was grateful to her guest. Olivia somehow managed to cut through the dark atmosphere in the street, though there was always that baseline of anxiety bubbling away in the back of Daphne's mind and pit of her stomach. Still, Olivia always had a way of taking the attention somewhere brighter and more positive in a way only she could. She had her tea even sweeter than Daphne did, too. It somehow suited her. Then again, everything she did seemed to suit her.

'This is nuts, Daph. Seriously, nuts. What's the news? Did they find the man who did it?'

'I haven't been told anything,' replied Daphne, feeling like she was completely in the dark.

'The cops are buzzing round outside, aren't they? Any hot ones?' Olivia was starting her way of moving the conversation from fear to fun.

'Honestly Liv, trust you. But actually, no, not really,' said Daphne as Olivia smiled back.

'You know you can always move back in. That room's still yours if you want it.' This time she meant it. Daphne thought back to the promises made to her mother. But also, she wasn't stupid.

'Maybe just until all this blows over. I'll let you know tomorrow.'

Daphne fell deep in distracted thought. This had to blow over soon. This kind of craziness never lasts for long. She'd made a promise to her mother about returning to the house, and she could still keep that later. But it would also feel like a backward step. She'd have to watch her friends carry on with the course she'd just dropped out of, and that would make her feel horribly inadequate. But on the flip side, no one there was being murdered.

'Hey!' smiled a patient Olivia. 'You'll be fine. You always are. Things always are. That's just how the world works.'

'I want Mum back.' A tear formed in Daphne's eye. 'What a way to treat a heartbroken girl, God or the

Universe or whoever is doing this to me. I'd be furious if I thought that stuff was real.'

The truth is she *was* furious. Why was she being treated like this? And because she didn't believe in God or the all-knowing Universe or the all-loving Pachamama or anything else, she had no one to be furious at. No one to blame and shout at. In a way, that was worse.

'Things will be fine,' replied Olivia. 'Always. Always, in the end.'

But things weren't fine, and that was confirmed by Angela Shipman on the TV news that evening as Daphne watched alone. An unusually shaken Shipman was reporting under lights with a background that looked a little too familiar.

'Further horrific news has come in from this already devastated community here on Hanging Hill Lane, where police have confirmed that four more suspicious deaths have taken place on the street, with some speculating that it happened inside the house next door to the previous deaths, currently being investigated as murders. This *is* just speculation at the moment and seems quite unlikely with the sheer amount of police in the area, one would think, but police haven't released any details and we'll bring them to you just as soon as they emerge.'

Ring ring... Daphne had used a vintage-style ringtone since she'd been away, matching it to her mother's old 1970s rotary dial as a way of having a constant reminder of home. But since she'd returned, that old phone hadn't rung once. Not a single call for her dead mother. Not one person who used to call so regularly had somehow missed the news of her passing and called. Daphne hadn't had to tell a soul. It was like everyone knew it had happened the second it did. Everyone except her.

She picked up her phone. It was Sara.

'Yeah, I'm watching,' said Daphne. 'Come on over.'

Daphne was grateful for the visit. Between Olivia, an occasional policeman and Sara and Alfie, she never felt too alone for long. Now it was Sara's turn to sit with her, both scared to death. Two multiple murders on the same street, just a few houses up from theirs. Only one house separated Sara from the new crime scene, and if true, the recently murdered family were known to them both.

'I'm so scared,' said Sara. 'Scared for little Alfie. What a world for him to grow up in.'

'It's a scary world,' replied Daphne. 'I'm scared. I'm scared all the time.'

'Something's going on with the family next door. I saw them out the window getting into a police car.'

Daphne didn't know what to make of that.

'Wait, they're your next-door-neighbours! Oh God, Sara. Do they think it was them?' Daphne had grown up with them, and they'd always seemed like a lovely family. Luke, the only son, was her age and they'd played together as kids. He'd even asked her out when they were fourteen and they'd gone on a little date. Now, the family she'd been so close to were being taken by the police for doing something so horrific, and she felt that in her gut like a forceful stab from the end of a broom handle. But then there was the slight sense of suspended relief. Is it over? Did they catch the murderer? All those thoughts flashed through in a second as her mind raced as fast as her heart. Was it them?

'I don't think so,' replied Sara. 'It didn't look that way. There's always police out there now. So many. I did wonder why so many arrived.'

Daphne was glad they were there. And then, out of nowhere, a loud bang.

It was another familiar sound of the house – the huge brass door knocker. Someone clearly preferred to knock and knock loud than press the little ding-dong button.

It was PC Knight, a new policeman to Daphne and an absolute mountain of a man. His biceps bulged out of his police-issue polo shirt, and Daphne, no stranger to measuring up humans, judged him to be up near seven feet tall. He was so big that Daphne took a moment to realise there was another, older man there too. He was smaller, in a smart suit with an identification lanyard around his neck, a calming presence and charm about him. He stepped forward lightly, dwarfed by the massive constable next to him.

'Can we come in?'

In the lounge, the policemen recognised Sara instantly. The older man sat down, the massive PC Knight in the doorway, blocking almost all the light from the hallway.

'Hello, I'm just here to introduce myself. I'm Detective Inspector Bright, in charge of this operation. I'd just like to let you know that we are doing absolutely everything possible to keep everybody safe and catch whoever did this.'

'Are they all dead?' Sara asked, clutching Alfie nervously. 'Both families?'

DI Bright looked up to PC Knight, and then back to Sara. The answer in his face was yes.

'I'm sorry, I'm unable to comment on specifics, but normally in cases like this the perpetrator and the victims are very well-known to each other, and we have absolutely no reason to believe that there is any kind of threat beyond what has happened. And that's all in the past now.'

That made sense to Daphne for a moment. The victims and killer would be known to each other, and the police had taken away the family from number six. But which one did it? Not Luke. He was so nice. So nice that Daphne had been put off a second date by the constant too-niceness of it all. But surely not Luke's mum. She was the most normal person on the street. Picture a harmless, ageing lady who has long abandoned makeup and doing anything remotely difficult or tiring, but would still go out of her way to help anyone in need, give her a slightly over-sized lower lip and droopy eyes, and you'll get an image of exactly what she looked like. She definitely wasn't a murderer. She wouldn't have had the energy if she'd wanted to be. The dad? He was a charity worker for a small animal shelter just beyond the woods. They were the nicest, most normal family in the world. And now they'd been taken by the police for killing nine people. Suddenly it didn't make sense anymore.

Someone was shuffling around behind the lounge doorway, obscured by the mighty PC Knight. DI Bright continued in his calming manner.

'This is PC Knight and PC Foot, two of the officers on this case. Just give them a shout if you need anything, or see or hear anything that might be of help.'

PC Foot, the kind officer who'd checked out the back garden looking for the woman in the tree, peered between the doorframe and the giant frame of PC Knight.

'Hello again,' PC Foot smiled nervously. 'No one out there but your neighbour Mrs Tamblyn on a walk.'

Mrs Tamblyn. Deanna? Could it have been Deanna Tamblyn in the tree? She was weird for sure, but not *that* weird, and surely not strong enough to climb a tree like that or scamper over the fence at the sign of an incoming policeman.

'You'll be safe with us,' said PC Knight in a voice with more authority than sound should be allowed to convey. Somehow that helped the girls believe it, though it woke little Alfie.

'Come on then, Casper,' said PC Knight to PC Foot, who seemed a little embarrassed to be called by his nickname in front of civilians, and the two left.

Before DI Bright stood up, he had one more thing to say, and said it with a little more authority than his normal calming voice.

'Just some advice for you. Don't go searching for news or information on the internet. Just keep yourselves occupied while we sort this all out. Try to have a good night.' He got up and left, leaving the two girls hugely unnerved.

'What did he have to go and say that for?' said Sara, annoyed.

Daphne didn't want to have anything to do with that comment.

'Don't do it,' she replied. 'I'm not doing it.'

And Alfie cried.

CHAPTER SIX

It wasn't until gone midnight that Daphne felt calm enough to sleep. She'd done some painting which had helped, and her new picture was becoming a little clearer. It was shaping up into some kind of animal, possibly a dog but maybe a cat or hare. She cleaned her teeth, which unusually produced some blood as she spat, and went to bed. A couple of hours later, she was asleep. Not sound asleep, but as close as could be expected. Daphne lay still and the world went quiet. Nothing but faint whispers of wind blowing over the chimney.

Nothing moving, nothing making a sound.

Nothing, but the quiet footsteps passing by outside in the dark.

Nothing. Nothing but stillness.

Nothing but a small snort of water from a tap. It stopped as quick as it started.

Nothing but a lightly sleeping, scared eighteen-year-old.

Nothing but three mannequins, dimly silhouetted by the streetlight outside, one rocking ever-so-gently.

Nothing. Until that damn alarm.

She was sure she'd turned it off, but today it was apparently set for an hour earlier than she would get up even on busy college days. She went back to sleep as best she could, only to be rudely awoken by the doorbell – that damn doorbell – not even an hour later.

She woke with a new feeling in her stomach. A feeling that something was badly wrong with her world in a way that words couldn't describe. Her dream hid away in an instant but it must have been a bad one to leave her with a deep, dark feeling like that. And now it felt like the doorbell was screaming in her face. After a night with barely any real sleep, it was a horrible decision she had to make. Can she ignore it and close her eyes again? What if she returns to that horrible dream that she could still sense lurking? What if the awful feeling is a warning not to answer the door? What if it's the police? If it's the police, she should answer. Who else might it be? No one's called. Must be the police. Dammit, better answer it. Damn doorbell.

It wasn't the police.

The spyhole revealed a big-built man with a scruffy shirt and an almost-bald head that looked as perfectly round as a pool ball. What did he want? He wasn't the police for sure. Not the God-Squad either, they always looked so much smarter, or at least they tried. The police must have let him through though, surely, so it must be safe. Maybe some civilian help or advisor. There was only one way to find out.

'Hi,' said the round head with a smile, holding up his camera just an inch or two. 'I was just wondering if I could have a little chat about the murders up the road, and maybe get a photo or two for the local paper?'

Press? *You've got to be kidding me!* Daphne had yanked herself out of bed for this, and there was no way she'd get back to sleep now. Another tired, stressful day was now certain, and all because of this, well, *selfish arsehole* were the words that went through Daphne's head and stopped just before they reached her mouth. She was good at stopping herself from speaking. Good at being invisible.

But stronger than the words she was thinking was the feeling in her whole body. The annoyance, the tiredness and constant anxiety, that bad feeling left over from the dream, were at that moment, merging and amplifying, twisting and churning together and turning into rage. How dare this man wake her up? Was it not obvious she would be tired and scared? She would have screamed and punched if only her conditioning had allowed it. But there was always one thing her mother would teach her and teach her again: you must be in control of your emotions. 'Hear them,' she used to say, 'but don't let them control you. They're an invitation to act, not your boss.' It was advice that had served Daphne well. Her mother was often cryptic in her advice, but on this, she was clear as a crystal.

'No thank you, I'm sorry,' she replied, not taking up the rage's invitation to shout but purposefully letting it strengthen her body to push the door firmly enough so she wouldn't be argued with. The man aggressively thrust his foot in the doorway at the last second, making it impossible to close. The rage's invitation got stronger.

'It'll only take a minute, it's just a few questions,' said the round-headed man with a calm smile that didn't at all match his foot, aggressively wedged against the door.

'No thank you!' shouted Daphne, the rage now starting to take control as she banged the door hard into his ankle in the hope he'd pull it away in pain. But that he did not do.

Daphne was a small girl and the man outsized her by many a pound, and he had no problem smashing the door back into the house and Daphne with it. It only took him half a second to raise his camera and get a couple of quick shots before Daphne charged back, throwing a slap and even a left-hand punch. This was no invitation acceptance. No RSVP. This was the rage taking over.

The man defended his face and camera as best he could as the strikes rained in before gently pushing her away and looking up, shocked.

'I'm trying to help you,' were the words he squeaked before Daphne shoulder-barged the door shut, the man flinching and pulling his foot out at the last minute to avoid a bruised shin or worse from this crazy girl.

Knock knock knock! The man wasn't giving up. The huge brass door knocker that so recently had been a comforting, nostalgic sound, had changed to something completely different for young Daphne, who breathed deeply, trying to rein in her rage. The adrenaline fuelling the rage didn't just disappear. Instead, it fuelled a different feeling. Her hands no longer shook with anger, but with fear. Knock knock knock! Bang bang bang!

But she trusted the old, hugely thick wooden door that had kept intruders out for more than a century, and the huge black metal lock that always looked like it would be a better fit in a medieval castle somewhere deeper into Europe, and even though this man was still right outside, things began to feel just a little better.

Knock knock knock knock!

Through the spyhole, Daphne watched the man pounding on the old heavy knocker, but instead of getting even more scared, or angry, she noticed quite the opposite. She noticed her trust in the thick wood, and how safe she felt in that old house, even if some idiot stranger was trying to pound down the door. If anything, the fish-eye lens effect of the spyhole combined with the roundness of this angry face, red from her slaps and punches, made him somehow look like an angry tomato, and she couldn't help but find it funny. What a truly beautiful and safe house she really lived in. And what a time to be needing a truly safe house. No one would ever get through that door without machinery or a few strong men and a battering ram – and that wasn't going to happen with all those police outside. Not that they'd been good for much. More scary to her than the man at the door was the thought that he might go directly to those policemen and accuse her of assault. He had a red face and she had scuffs and grazes on her knuckles and there would be no denying it.

The angry tomato gave up, checking his camera screen at the doorway before he left, flicking through the rushed shots, and ran off quickly out of sight.

Red hair shining, there she was. Revealed by the intruder's tomato head moving out of the way, at the other side of the road, as always, was Morwenna Rowe, appearing to look right back through the spyhole at Daphne.

Daphne darted back. There's always that moment in between instinct and logic, where instinct wins the race and makes you flinch and your heart jump, and then the logic follows and you wonder what on earth you were doing. Of course she couldn't be seen. A second later, Daphne put her eye back to the spyhole – and jolted back again, heart racing harder, her hand over her mouth trying to stifle a scream and quieten her loud breathing.

Right outside the spyhole, not six inches away, looking straight back in, was Morwenna Rowe. That was impossible. She'd been on the other side of the road, a good forty feet away. But there she was, a second or two later. It was definitely her, yet couldn't have been. And she'd definitely seen back through the spyhole because she'd jumped and jolted too as if she'd been surprised herself.

This was too much. Daphne sank to the floor. She trusted that old secure door, and an old lady like Morwenna Rowe certainly wasn't going to push it open, but that new junk spyhole clearly wasn't stopping her from seeing in, and the floor was a sure blind spot.

Daphne sat, listening, waiting to hear footsteps outside leaving.

Silence.

Was she still out there? A great, five-inch-thick wooden door was perfect to stop intruders, but it was also very difficult to hear through. And if there was one thing Daphne was not going to do it was check through that spyhole, which she'd just found out horribly wasn't one-way after all.

A crawl down the corridor and around the corner into the lounge would keep her in the blind spot, she thought, and she stayed on all fours until she'd reached the lounge entrance. After a minute to catch her breath, hoping the very strange lady would be gone, she walked quickly into the kitchen and picked up her phone.

But Daphne's heart rate wasn't given a chance to rest. In the back garden, standing by a large burning bonfire bellowing black smoke, was Gugwana, staring straight back at her.

Who starts a fire in someone's back garden? Dementia is a strange and horrible thing. Eventually, you don't even know who you are.

That poor old lady. Under normal circumstances, Daphne would have been straight outside to check on and keep safe this old family friend, once so happy and switched on, but now clearly in the later and saddest stages of dementia. She must have still had her old physical strength, mind, to get over that fence. Normally, under normal times, Daphne would've been straight out to fix things. Normally. Under normal times. But today, she was scared, angry, and with a deep feeling that something awful was about to happen. That dream still hadn't fully left her. It would be a long time until it did.

A bucket of water takes a while to fill, and Gugwana had disappeared. Back over the fence one presumes, unless she was so far gone into madness she'd decided to disappear into the fire and self-immolate.

The back door leading to the garden was as thick and secure as the front, and although Daphne had never questioned it, she was now noticing these things. She'd once asked her mother if the windows were double-glazed after a salesman had popped by. 'More than that, dear, more than that,' her mother had replied, leaving Daphne with the impression for years that they had triple-glazed windows, maybe or maybe not as good as bullet-proof, perhaps, but enough to stop a senile old lady or intrusive reporter.

It wasn't until the tap stopped running and the racket of water hitting water stopped that she noticed her phone ringing on the side by the black iron stovetop and the time-worn kettle. It was Sara calling, and Daphne had never been happier to see her name. The five minutes it took her to arrive felt like an eternity to Daphne, who threw the bucket of water on the fire and was surprised to see the whole thing extinguish in one, with a final puff of steam and smoke jetting up the moment the water hit. Perhaps a gust of wind had hit it at just the right time and blown out the rest as the water landed, but it still didn't seem right. Nothing did. As she stepped back through the door into the kitchen, the coldness seemed to step in behind her.

She secured the back door with its big black old key and put the steel bar across it. That was something else that was just accepted as normal as a kid – putting a huge iron bar with beautiful inscriptions across the back door – but seemed a little strange after returning from living in a couple of modern houses where people were happy to flick a flimsy key round halfway and leave the rest to trust. She hadn't bothered with it since being home, but now she thought it would be best. Her mother really was a stickler for security wasn't she, perhaps to the point she might have been diagnosed with something if she'd ever seen a psychologist. But the obsession with security was now paying off, and Daphne realised just how grateful she really was for her mother and everything she'd done for her. Even after death, she was still protecting her, as if she knew that this might one day happen. She couldn't have done though. Nothing had ever happened on Hanging Hill Lane, least of all something so big and brutal as two multiple murders. With steam or smoke still coming from the ashes, Daphne refilled the bucket, ready for if it started to burn again.

The sound of the doorbell, even when she knew it was her friend, now made Daphne feel nervous. She could feel her heart boom as soon as the first tone struck. Still, at least the bell didn't sound as aggressive as that big old brass knocker. Even the spyhole now made her nervous to get too close to, but she did anyway. She knew it would be Sara, but didn't want any nasty surprises. She'd had quite enough of those and that baseline of permanent anxiety was creeping upwards, and downwards into her legs which now shook a little whenever someone was at the door. Perhaps Tomato had gone to the police and it was them. The relief on confirming it was Sara and Alfie was huge.

The two made themselves comfortable, physically at least, and Daphne relayed what had happened to her already that morning. The intrusive press man. The weirdness of Morwenna Rowe. The terribly sad story of Gugwana.

'There are so many police out there now,' Sara said. 'It's really getting to me. And I'm so tired with Alfie. I've never known tiredness like it. It's true what they say about newborns.'

'Me too, I'm exhausted,' replied Daphne, sparking some visible annoyance in Sara, who in her awfully tired state thought she somehow had the monopoly on exhaustion. How could anyone without a baby be as tired as her?

'You can't be that tired,' was what came out of her mouth, triggering annoyance in Daphne now too, and tension started to creep into the room. Invisible, but very much there. She had just as much reason to be tired. Even without the weirdness and aggressive visitors, she was still grieving with a very open wound. But for such a young woman, she was well-trained with her emotions, even if she had just lost control ten minutes before. Just an invitation, that annoyance was. A tempting invitation of course. Tempting to snap back at someone who just judged her for being tired when she had every right and reason to be. But Daphne's mother had taught her well, so she let the annoyance subside, noticing how truly emotionally ruined Sara really looked. She was completely beaten, and the feeling turned to sympathy for her old friend.

'Are you coping okay?' she asked, banishing the dark tension from the house.

'I'm surviving, somehow. That cocky policeman told me they took next door into protection. Luke's dad demanded it and wouldn't take no for an answer. Thought if this is some weird serial killer they might be next.'

'Should we go too? Into police protection?' asked Daphne, wondering if police protection might be better than her five-inch wooden door.

'I already have it, that's what he told me. There's police all around here now. Officer Cocky said they think they'll catch him soon, so I guess that's good.'

'They know it's a him?' asked Daphne.

'I guess?' replied Sara. 'You think it's a woman?'

'There are some strange women around here, you know that,' said Daphne. 'I just don't know. No one knows anything and it's stressing me out. I just need something, you know. Something to make me feel better.'

'I've got something,' Sara said, trying to smile but just looking more exhausted.

'You know something?' Daphne perked up.

'No. I have something.' Sara reached into her bag and brought out a framed photo of her and baby Alfie, who was wearing the cow onesie that Daphne had made. 'It's just a home print. I've been too busy to get a proper one done. He loves it, thank you.'

Daphne took it with a smile over to the shelf.

'Look, it's almost the same.' She picked up a photo of herself as a baby being held by her own mother, in a very similar frame on the mantlepiece. It was uncanny. The position of the people in the photos, the hats the adults were wearing, the corner of the doors in the background just poking into the shot behind the mothers' left shoulders. The only real difference was the clothes. Daphne's mother wore a T-shirt that read in red text, for a reason she never knew nor really even considered, *They're coming.* The poses were slightly different too. While Sara looked at baby Alfie in her shot, Daphne's mother was looking straight at the lens as if trying to signal something.

She was about to hold up the photos side by side to show Sara the remarkable resemblance when instead her heart rate shot up again, reacting to that damn doorbell, now conditioned into her brain as an unnerving Pavlovian response. *Who this time?* Her right knee gave a little shake.

Though reluctant to use the ineffective spyhole that now made her nervous, it was still a better option than opening the door blind. On the doorstep, bent out of shape by the fish-eye lens effect, was Timothy and his short friend, waiting patiently. It was a relief if anything, at least it wasn't a knock from the police for slapping that aggressive tomato out the door. But Daphne was never going to answer this, not if she lived to a thousand years. The weird thing was though, although Timothy's eyes occasionally glanced over the spyhole, it not once seemed like he could see in. But if Timothy couldn't, how could Morwenna Rowe? Daphne gave Timothy a little wave through it. Nothing. The God-Squad gave up and left, walking back down the road towards the woodland. How could that be? Did Timothy have bad eyes? Could Morwenna see nothing and it had just seemed like she could? After plenty of time for Timothy to get clear, she slowly opened the door, peering out into the road, and saw the coast was clear. Just police cars and plenty of officers and a friendly hopping hare. She stepped outside, pushed the door closed a little, and looked back through her spyhole. She couldn't see a thing until her eye was right up against it. That gave her confidence in it after all. It worked just fine. As for Morwenna, who knows what that was about. Just her being a weird old lady, maybe, was Daphne's clutch for normality as she returned to her lounge where Sara waited, almost falling asleep.

'Seriously, Sara,' she said as she sat. 'So many creeps and weirdos round here.'

'Just the one I'm worried about,' replied Sara. 'You know, the one who's been killing and all that.'

'I'm being serious though,' said Daphne. 'God botherers, the photographer, but that's not even the really weird thing. Not even Gugwana out the back was the weirdest, poor lady.'

'Oh?' asked Sara.

'It's Morwenna Rowe. I've seen her do some weird things. You know, and you're not going to believe this, but...' but Sara wasn't listening. 'What's wrong Sara? You're struggling aren't you.' Daphne offered a hug but Sara pushed it gently away, a tear forming in her eye.

'The family from number eight. I saw them. I shouldn't have looked.'

'What do you mean?' asked Daphne, trying to show sympathy but starting to feel nervous as a different kind of dark feeling flowed into the room. Invisible, but very much there.

'On the internet. Pictures. He was right, I shouldn't have looked.'

As the colour started to drain away from Sara's face right in front of Daphne's eyes, her heart rate jumped again with her horrible new Pavlovian response. That damned doorbell!

'Wait there Sara,' Daphne said with affection and sympathy. 'Let me deal with that. Honestly, I'm going to rip that thing down soon.'

The perfectly functioning one-way spyhole revealed the man in charge of the police presence again, DI Bright, flanked by PC Foot and PC Lamb. *Shit.* She was in trouble now. Her mother was right. Control your emotions, otherwise you'll get in trouble. Okay. Deep breath. Let's get this over with.

When Daphne opened the door, DI Bright no longer had that calming persona or that perfectly controlled, tension-dissolving voice. He was like a different man. He looked at Daphne as if looking right through her, and PC Foot almost had to remind him to speak, so long was the pause. Daphne's heart rate raced faster as she prepared to tell her side of the story.

'I'm going to have to ask you to stay inside until further notice, while we deal with what's outside.'

'Sure,' replied Daphne, with DI Bright's visible fear starting to attach itself to her too in a way that it was set to cling to her for quite some time. 'What's going on?'

'I can't say right now. I'm sorry.' PC Lamb looked like he was going to be sick as Sara appeared at the door behind Daphne.

'Miss Hunter,' continued DI Bright. 'I'm going to place you under protection tonight, and the child. There's nothing to worry about.'

Daphne didn't believe that, and she could tell the man speaking, the head of the police protection in the area, didn't either. Bright continued, 'I'll station cars front and back tonight, with armed officers in each. Officers on the road and patrolling the woods. I'll assign you officers inside your house too, Miss Hunter, just to be sure, as part of the protection. Just to make sure you're absolutely safe.' His once so calm voice had actually cracked on those last two words, and Daphne didn't believe a word of it.

'Yes please,' said Sara, holding Alfie so tight he started to cry. 'Who was the big policeman who was here? Can I have him? The massive guy.'

PC Lamb stuttered into the conversation, still looking like he was trying not to throw up.

'PC Kn-Knight, PC Knight isn't–'

But Bright cut him off before he could finish.

'PC Knight isn't available tonight, he was on late duties last night I'm afraid.'

But PC Lamb was visibly cracking. 'PC Knight isn't unavailable. He's not there. He hasn't spoken, He's a shell, just a shell. Go on, tell them!'

But DI Bright had no intention to, and snapped hard. 'PC Lamb!'

'Tell them about Rob, too.' Lamb turned to Daphne.

'Rob, that was here. Remember him? The DS?' The girls looked horrified as Lamb looked back to DI Bright. 'Go on, tell them. This is their lives, they should know.'

'PC Lamb get in the car right now!'

But Lamb wasn't stopping. 'He's not the only officer to kill himself this week, is he sir?'

That was enough for DI Bright, trying desperately to regain some kind of control over the situation.

'Casper!' ordered Bright. 'Get him out of here.'

PC 'Casper' Foot firmly led Lamb away towards a car. He broke into childlike tears before he'd taken his third step. Two officers approached as if to replace them.

Bright did his best to reassure the girls, turning his attention to Daphne.

'You're alone?'

Daphne nodded, wanting to know more, but a part of her forbade her from asking through fear of what she might find out.

'These chaps are with you, Miss Hunter,' continued Bright. 'You can go with them now please.'

Daphne was horrified to see her best friend leave like that, holding a tiny baby and with two police officers, both of whom were clearly putting on brave faces.

'Don't worry, you'll be safe,' said Bright to Daphne.

'I want protection too,' pleaded Daphne, visibly shaking.

'We're stretched here. Really stretched.'

'I want protection!' demanded Daphne, refusing to be overlooked, accepting the invitation from her fear to push harder. Bright looked back at her, considering it intensely like he was somehow fighting himself inside.

'Okay. PC Foot will be around shortly, he will stay with you as long as you want him to. I'm sorry.'

DI Bright turned and left, leaving Daphne feeling utterly terrified and completely alone. That five inches thick wooden door suddenly felt very thin. But it wasn't until she saw the photograph on the floor by her feet that she finally felt true terror for the first time. She'd have screamed, if only she wasn't too terrified for any of her vocal muscles to move.

The photograph was of her, in her own doorway, pushing back towards the camera, from the point of view of a rude round-headed photographer. But that wasn't the worrying part. The worrying part, the part that scared and shook her to her core, was in the background behind her. That part was what made her realise she hadn't been living alone in that house. That was the part that terrified her more than anything else that had been happening.

That part almost broke her. That part was staring at her. That part was the eyes.

CHAPTER SEVEN

Daphne sat in her lounge with two men she'd recently met but never expected in her life she'd be making tea for with her mum's old whistling kettle.

PC Foot, or Casper as he'd been called a couple of times now, had been assigned to stay with her. Attached to a radio connected to an army of police fit for a war right outside, his presence made Daphne feel a little better, but not much. Whatever that was in the photograph, all the police in the world couldn't protect her from. For that, she'd turned to a man of God.

Timothy hadn't had milk in his tea, such is the American way, and the small teacup somehow didn't seem to fit his tall, gangly frame. His fat friend wasn't there. PC Foot only allowed one visitor at a time for everyone's safety. One man he could handle, but two added a little extra risk he wasn't willing to take. He wasn't an armed officer but between his baton and chemical pepper spray, if this man of God turned out to be a problem, he'd make things okay again very quickly.

The photograph lay on the table, equidistant between all three. They were eyes in the background for sure, but what kind of creature did they stare out from? It wasn't a dog or a cat, and the back half of the creature seemed to fade into nothing. That kind of thing happens when a camera is in jerky motion when the shutter snaps, and the tomato who took the photo was in a rush for sure, but the rest of the image was almost completely clean and perfectly sharp. It just didn't make sense. Not to Daphne, and not to Foot. But Timothy had a fair idea.

'You're not going to want to hear this,' said Timothy to Daphne. 'There's a war coming. This whole thing is their first play, and it's a clever one.'

Foot looked interested.

'What war? Whose play?' he asked.

Daphne was more confused than ever.

'You can't let them win. Let me find him,' said Timothy. 'Let me send him packing. Let's end this for all of you. Let me let the Saviour save you and everyone else.'

This man was making her uncomfortable, and she'd have been terrified had it not been for the police constable, even if he was picking at his fingernails nervously. But there was also the issue of the photograph. The photograph, and the eyes, and no other chance of any kind of explanation or solution. She had nothing to lose.

'Go ahead,' she said, slightly surprising Foot as he picked up his milky tea.

Timothy pulled out a large golden cross from his inside jacket pocket as he stood, holding it up and slowly turning.

'Don't worry,' he said to Daphne without looking. 'They've singled you out, but it's a small one. A powerful one wouldn't have shown up in a photo like that.'

Daphne and Foot looked at each other, Foot rolling his eyes but Daphne not in the mood for even a quick smile.

'Reveal yourself, demon! Reveal yourself and be sent back to where you came,' demanded Timothy cheesily with a determined face and some sweat starting to form on his forehead. He looked at Daphne. 'Wait here. I was born for this moment,' he said, cocksure, and walked out of the lounge.

PC Foot stood to follow but Daphne gestured for him to sit down. Whatever this was either had nothing to do with them or couldn't be helped by a can of pepper spray and a police-issue baton. She desperately hoped for the former. Or, more likely, Timothy was just another nutcase on the street. As mad as a box of frogs, her mother always used to say.

A mix of Timothy's voice and footsteps echoed back through the old house and into the lounge, getting more distant as he went.

'You'll have to do better than that, little demon. It is I, Timothy, and I come for you now.'

Daphne and PC Foot listened together, slightly unnerved but more confused, with Daphne considering if rumours of the supernatural had hit the street and this already strange religious fellow had happily dived directly down the rabbit hole.

'Reveal yourself and leave, little demon, leave this world now! Reveal yourself, and leave!'

Timothy's voice was getting louder, with growing confidence and authority. He was either saving mankind or was an absolute fruitcake, almost certainly the latter. 'Be gone, demon, be gone!'

And then, for a moment, quiet. No footsteps, no ramblings of an American madman.

Nothing.

Nothing but three mugs of tea on the table, all going cold.

Nothing but the sound of two humans breathing in the quiet house with the thick stone walls.

Nothing but the hiss of the speaker on the police comms radio, three motionless mannequins towering behind the man in uniform.

Nothing until Timothy's voice was heard once again, quieter, slower, but firm and confident.

'So there you hide.'

A smash from the kitchen. The old kettle suddenly sounded so loud it was more like a steam train blowing its whistle through a tunnel. Another smash. A crash. A rumble. And then nothing.

Nothing but the sound of PC Foot slowly standing, drawing his baton, looking utterly terrified, pale as a ghost, and a smell flooding into the room that reminded Daphne of the time they'd found that dead black cat beneath the floorboards a whole hot summer after one from a neighbouring street had disappeared. It was vile.

It was the literal smell of death, and it was somehow being overpowered by the silence of where there had just been so much sound.

And then the silence gave way. Footsteps. Footsteps running, getting louder, getting closer, from the kitchen and through the hall, and a quick flash of beansprout Timothy running at speed past the lounge door. The front door clicked open, and the sounds of the footsteps disappeared into the outside air. On the floor, right outside the lounge door, lay something that had fallen as he fled. The cross remained, but the man of God was most definitely gone.

PC Foot was on the radio calling for assistance with one hand and slowly raising his baton with the other, cautiously edging towards the lounge door. Daphne sat, confused, scared, watching. Within seconds, police piled into the house. Five, then ten, then almost twenty. But all they found was a smashed jar of elderberry jam and a kettle over a hot flame but with no water inside. It was an hour before they'd all departed, having checked every corner of every room in that old house. But they'd found nothing. Nothing strange at all.

Nothing but three mannequins standing side by side in the lounge.

Nothing but a half-finished painting of some kind of animal in the bedroom.

Nothing but a damp pile of ash in the back garden, still steaming.

Nothing that seemed odd at all.

Nothing weird or off. Until darkness fell, and evening swept in.

***

Daphne and Foot had just been having a friendly chat, trying to pretend to themselves that things were normal and their world was all okay. PC Foot had revealed his name as Andrew, and to Daphne, was no longer just a friendly man in a uniform with a radio and a metal stick, but a fellow human being who was frightened but doing his best. And as all fellow humans need to do, he'd disappeared off to use the bathroom. It was then when things started to get weird.

Across the room by the window, the wind began to whistle. That wasn't unusual in that old house, especially when the wind got up in just the wrong direction. But it was normally just sounds, and no breeze inside. So why did the door creak open a little when Andrew was long gone? Why were the mannequins swaying gently? And why did Daphne's hair move several inches in the breeze she couldn't even feel? That was enough to send a shiver right down her spine and get the skin on her forehead tingling, a horrible feeling that would've been utterly terrifying had the sound of the wind not coincided with it and provided at least some sort of rational explanation. She felt freezing cold too, another sign of fear – or so she thought, until Andrew got back.

'It's suddenly cold in here,' he said, putting on his police-issue fleece and sitting back down on the sofa that would become his bed for the night. Daphne couldn't bear to give him her mother's bed. She couldn't even go in that room. Not yet.

Daphne tried to paint to rest her mind before she attempted to sleep, but couldn't. Her mind was on other things. The murders, the behaviour of Timothy, the strange ladies. But it wasn't long until her mind turned to her mother. In her whole life, this was the time she needed her the most, and she wasn't there and never again would be. This was the exact moment that that fact, for the very first time, really hit home.

She'd been so distracted since the news of her death that she hadn't had time to really feel it. But grief always catches up, however hard we try to, or are forced to, put it off. This was the very moment it truly arrived. Poor Daphne could've pinpointed the exact three seconds her heart pulled itself into pieces, finally truly realising that her mother was gone and wasn't coming back. Throughout all of this mess, she realised, was the strange half-hope that she'd appear back home and make everything okay again, just like she had done so many times before. But that wasn't going to happen. She was gone forever. No amount of painting could help her feel better from that. All she did was lie on her bed, and cry. And cry and cry and cry. And eventually, for the first time in a long time, she fell into a deep sleep. Finally, in that sleep, she didn't feel scared. She felt nothing. Nothing at all.

Nothing. Nothing was happening in that quiet house.

Nothing but a sleeping teenager, alone in her bed.

Nothing but a half-sleeping policeman, alone on the sofa, with his black hat over his face.

Nothing but two thick wooden old doors, bolted shut, secure and safe.

Nothing but a kitchen knife falling from the hanging rack and clattering on the hard stone floor.

Nothing but a sleepy policeman, checking on the noise and putting the knife back on the kitchen top.

Nothing but the light whistle of the wind and the soft light of the moon.

Nothing but three mannequins, gently and slowly rocking.

Nothing but Daphne's bed cover slowly pulling itself off her, and a teenage girl yanking it hard with frustration back up to her chin without waking.

And then from that nothing, the whispers came.

It was the first night terror Daphne had had in years, and the most terrifying. Her eyes flicked open, staring straight up into the dark, the faintest of moonlight coming through the window. Daphne would have jumped and screamed if only any of her muscles had awoken with her. Whispering right into her left ear started the first voice.

'Hello, Miss Locke.'

Her whole body stiffened and cramped as she felt the most disgusting feeling, as if something damp slid across her cheek and ear. It felt like it was being licked by a dog, but very slowly and with an awful smell. But there was no dog there. No rough but wet warty tongue. There was nothing.

'First, we killed the five at number ten,' whispered the voice.

A second voice started into her right ear.

'The four at eight were next to die, and then...'

The first sounded proud of itself as it whispered again.

'The three at six we nailed to the door.'

It laughed.

The second voice slowed it right down, taunting.

'I hooked and pulped the two who died at four.'

Sara. Alfie.

'Now it's time for us to come for you.'

The wet, slow, sliding feeling returned, up across and into her ear, licked by something that smelled of death.

'You stupid little single girl, alone at number two.'

That word *stupid* had been the worst of them all. It had been the word on which the whisper turned, becoming a full-throated voice from the darkness. *Stupid.* The word seemed like it came as much from the centre of her brain as an inch outside her head, somehow both omnipresent and targeted straight into her, sharp and penetrating like a spitting-hot sewing needle through an eardrum. If anyone had designed anything to terrify a lone girl, that very word would have been it.

And then the eyes appeared. Inches from Daphne's own unblinking eyes were the eyes from the photograph, looking straight down at her. Daphne lay still, terrified, shaking and completely unable to move. Paralysed. Then the voice spoke again.

'You. Will. Burn.'

And then the eyes disappeared, and there was nothing.

Nothing but the quilt flinging itself off the bed and the temperature suddenly dropping so low Daphne could see her fast breath approaching hyperventilation.

And then, again, nothing. Nothing but a terrified teenager shivering, alone and ready to crack. Nothing else at all.

Nothing but faint, soft moonlight. Nothing.

Until morning came, and with it, the next part of their plan.

CHAPTER EIGHT

A night terror.

That's what Daphne had put the last night's weird experience down to. The other options didn't bear thinking about. Was she losing her mind? Was something in the room with her? That thought was just too scary for her to let linger. If left to fester, it would grow and feed on her sanity until she had none left. It would breed and multiply with her other fears and insecurities and take over her mind entirely. It would be like the last, solitary light left inside her head would be left to fight an army of her own making. She'd been there once before. She had to dispatch that thought, now.

She hadn't had night terrors for a long time, but it made sense that they had returned now, with all the new and strange stress. If only her mother had been around to come in and chase the terror away like the olden days when she often used to dream of burning to death.

But without her mother, there was still a trick left that she remembered. Every time the dark, fearful mood from the nightmares lingered into the morning and threatened the day, it could always be washed away with a nice long hot shower.

Today, that very nearly worked.

Daphne, like nearly everyone else, had the same shower routine every time. Hers involved putting her towel on top of the laundry basket so she could easily reach around the curtain and grab it after turning off the water, and dry off a little before she got out. Today was exactly the same as the last four hundred showers she'd taken. Apart from one thing.

As she reached around the curtain and put her hand on the towel, something was different. On top of the towel, there was something cold and hard. She pulled back the curtain. It was the photo of Sara and Alfie, now with a huge crack down the middle of the glass.

Who'd put that there?

Wrapping herself in her towel, she tried the door to see if it was unlocked. Maybe PC Foot had broken it and was confessing as soon as possible, though that would be a bit weird, walking into the bathroom like that. Except the door was locked.

'Andrew!' she called. 'Someone's been in here.'

Minutes later, Daphne stood in her lounge, her house once again crawling with police officers. DI Bright stood alongside a large armed officer with a huge beard, and an approachable-looking young female officer. Daphne was close to tears. Not one of the police officers looked like they had any idea what was going on. Many looked scared. A couple looked completely terrified.

'There's no way at all it could have got in there?' Bright asked Daphne as she shivered in her towel.

'I keep telling you,' Daphne said, frustrated. 'It was over there next to the photo of Mum. Please check Sara's okay, please.'

'Lyons, Harmann,' ordered Bright, some confidence returning to his voice. 'Go next door please and check everything is okay.'

Lyons, the armed officer with the beard, looked scared. 'Me, sir?'

'Now please Lyons,' ordered Bright, his patience wearing thin. 'Daphne, we've checked your room and it's secure. This is Jo, she's going to sit with you in your room while you get dressed, okay?'

It was the youngest police officer who first saw it. As Daphne was busy getting dressed, PC Joanne Bach was looking at the half-finished painting up on the easel, wondering who in the world had a taste in art quite that dark. It gave her the creeps more than any picture she'd ever seen before.

The animal, still neither dog nor cat, had the creepiest eyes she'd ever seen, and the back of the animal faded into nothing. As Daphne looked to see what had stolen PC Bach's attention, she stopped dead. Her heart almost beat right out of her chest. She was looking at her painting, except it wasn't her work. The creature, the cat she knew she'd been painting, was no longer a cat. It was now the creature with the terrifying eyes from the photograph.

As the police cleared the building deeming it safe and secure, Daphne thought about that painting, now face-down on the carpet so she didn't have to see it. She knew she was painting an animal. She knew her mind wandered miles into the past and future as she painted. She knew she was under huge stress with the most terrible things happening on her very street. A rational mind would put all that together and conclude that she'd done it in the later stages of tiredness and not realised. But she was sure she hadn't. Yet any alternative explanation was terrifying. The only way to stay sane was to pretend to herself that she believed the rational explanation. She well knew she didn't.

The last to leave was Andrew Foot, who'd kindly overstayed his shift to make sure Daphne was okay until everyone had gone. It was now mid-morning and Daphne's personal police protection wouldn't be back until darkness threatened again. Daphne knew Andrew was scared, and had done his very best not to show it to make her feel safe. It hadn't worked, but it was better than being left alone. She saw him to the door, grateful.

Andrew walked off towards an unmarked car as a police helicopter flew low overhead, taking Daphne's attention. That was until she was made to jump, which was now happening all too easily, by a lady appearing right beside her, her face just inches away. With her long grey hair, she was instantly recognisable as Deanna Tamblyn, the strange woman so often seen standing as still as a stone at the top of the hill, whose warm dirty breath Daphne could now feel on her cheek.

'Did he get inside you?' asked Deanna Tamblyn, with a disturbingly serious tone.

'What?' was all Daphne could say. She hadn't for one minute seen Andrew in that way, and found the idea almost as disgusting as Deanna Tamblyn's phrasing. He was older, and there as professional protection. He hadn't looked for a second like he was thinking that way. Yet this woman, another crazy from the street, had jumped straight to that conclusion. Not that it was anything to do with her.

'You mustn't let him get inside you,' said Deanna, as Daphne watched Andrew climb into a car. 'Believe me, he will try, and he will try soon.'

'I have to go,' replied Daphne, creeped out yet again and darting back into her house, closing the big thick door behind her.

The doorbell rang. Deanna wasn't giving up. It rang again and again. That damn doorbell had plagued her since she'd moved back and now it was relentless. Ding dong, ding dong. The sound was making Daphne angry, and not stopping. Ding dong. Who pressed a doorbell like that? Over and over again. Ding dong, ding dong. That damn doorbell! Ding dong ding dong. Ding dong ding dong. That was too much. If Deanna Tamblyn wasn't going, then the doorbell was, and Daphne reached up and yanked the speaker box off the wall, throwing it to the floor and watching the batteries bounce and roll across the carpet. But that wasn't enough to feed the anger she felt, so she gave it a good stamp too, smashing the case and yanking a couple of wires from their solder where they hung out the side and came to rest. How rude of that stupid woman. The whole thing had been rude, from her questions to the doorbell. At least the rude tomato head had given her some kind of amusement, but Deanna Tamblyn, she was just as rude as she was mad.

A check through the spyhole showed no one. Deanna Tamblyn had finally gone. But as Daphne walked back towards her kitchen, she was struck by a horrible, horrible realisation.

She was alone.

***

In a time not so long ago, there had been two people who Daphne could always count on for anything every single time, but that number had recently been reduced to one. The one who remained alive was Olivia, and she was around as fast as her open-topped car would carry her. Refused entrance to the street, she had parked in the car park by the woods and walked in the bottom way. She had talked her way through the police line in a typical Olivia fashion, and arrived with her normal smile and ability to make everything feel just a little better. But she could tell something was seriously wrong. Not just from the body language of the officers on the street, but by the fact that not one of the guys in uniform had checked her out. She wasn't used to that, and though she'd been waiting for it to happen, checking her peripheral vision for confirmation, it hadn't. There was something far more important on the minds of the scared humans in uniform than a pretty girl walking by, however short her shorts were. *I bet if I hummed a little tune they'd look*, thought one part of Olivia's brain. *You're so vain*, snapped another.

'I'm so worried about Sara and Alfie,' said Daphne as Olivia sat. It was true, but she was now far more worried about herself. Sara was under full protection and wasn't dealing with night terrors and a mind that was slowly cracking and seeing, hearing and feeling weird things that just couldn't be real. Daphne was starting to doubt her own sanity. Maybe Deanna and Gugwana weren't the crazies. Maybe *she* was. But she'd never let that on.

'What's going on then?' asked Olivia. 'I've seen the news and it looks so bad. But the rumours, are they true?' She dropped her car keys and phone on the table, settling in for a while.

'What rumours?' Daphne asked, not entirely wanting to hear.

'That three houses of people are all dead, and the bodies have been ripped to pieces. All cut up.'

'That's not true,' replied Daphne. 'It's two houses, and I haven't heard anything about people in pieces. Rumours get so stupid. But honestly, they don't tell me anything. I don't know what I'm allowed to say, but the third house got taken into protection. Which is good. They're good friends. They're okay. They're fine,' she said, realising she had no idea if they were fine or not.

'You know a lot for someone who doesn't get told anything,' said Olivia. 'I'm going to go out there and see what I can find out.'

Before Daphne realised she wanted to object, Olivia was off looking for gossip, opening the door to a policeman who walked in and closed the door behind him. His six-foot frame surprised Daphne as he walked into the lounge. But he was a welcome sight.

'Hey, I'm back,' said Andrew Foot.

'Hi Casper,' replied Daphne, wondering what kind of reaction that might get.

'Andrew is fine,' he said, slightly embarrassed, almost managing to not show it.

'Why do they call you Casper, Andrew?' she asked.

'No reason,' Andrew said, though he clearly knew there was. He suddenly looked deeply nervous.

'Oh, okay,' said Daphne, backtracking to help quell his discomfort. Andrew had always looked a little nervous, but she'd assumed it was because of the situation. Perhaps he had some kind of anxiety condition. Still, his secrecy somehow reminded her of Deanna Tamblyn's weird warning, through some bizarre invisible train of thought. And now there was a weird pause happening, with a little tension creeping into the room. Enough time for Daphne to start thinking new thoughts. Could Andrew have left the photo in the bathroom after all? Is he behind this somehow? The thought was terrifying.

'It took me years to join the force,' Andrew said, wanting to offer something to fill the awkward silence. 'I spent ten years as a community support officer trying to get in. I think sometimes that's how they still see me. And some of them are just cocky lads, maybe.'

'Not today,' said Daphne, pointing out a horrible truth.

'Perhaps,' said Andrew. 'But I won't let anyone hurt you. Whoever's doing this, we won't let them get close. I'll be right here with you.'

'No one could get into Sara's last night, could they?' Daphne asked, seeing the broken photo frame up next to the photo of her as a baby.

'She wasn't home,' said Andrew. 'She was taken into hiding. They didn't tell anyone that though. About four of us knew. There was no way they were being found. She's still in a secret and safe place, I'm sure. I don't know where.'

There was a light rat-a-tat-tat on the door, the same knock Olivia had used when she'd arrived, and had used at the shared house whenever she'd forgotten her key. With no doorbell, no loud knocker and a friendly familiar tapping, it was the first time someone had been at the door for a while in a way that hadn't got Daphne's automatic nervous defences up. But still, she checked the spyhole anyway, just in case. Olivia looked shaken as they walked back into the lounge.

'I shouldn't have asked,' said Olivia, worried in a way Daphne had never seen her before.

'What did you find out? What won't they tell me?' Daphne now needed to know, but Andrew shook his head, trying to get Olivia to keep quiet. She didn't care.

'The family from number six, they're all dead,' she said, shaking. 'They got taken into protection and all ended up dead. The policemen with them killed themselves. No one knows what happened. They got followed.'

Daphne was shocked. It would take a while to sink in. Luke. The lovely parents. All gone. But there was something more urgent than grieving for a family of old friends. The third house had confirmed the pattern. Number ten, dead. Eight, dead. Now number six, all dead. If the night terror voices were real and right, next would be Sara and Alfie at four. And then her, the stupid little single girl alone at number two. And no one had been able to do a damn thing about it.

'Poor Luke,' Daphne said, still thinking about the danger to herself.

'They were found at their house. They were taken into protection but found back at home, dead.' Olivia was almost in tears, such was the shock. 'They were nailed to their own front door. I saw the blood.' She choked on almost every one of those last words.

Daphne was silent, unable to say a word.

'How could you let this happen?' cried Olivia, looking at Andrew. 'Idiots!' She reached down and picked up her car keys and phone. Daphne stood. She couldn't stay here. She'd be waiting to either die or go mad, and she wasn't up for either of those things. It was a different world over at Olivia's. One where things were fun and made sense.

'I don't want to be here,' said Olivia, finding her car key on the ring.

'Wait, Liv, I'm going to come with you. Still okay to stay, yeah?'

Olivia had never let her down, and if the police couldn't protect her in her house or anywhere else, she wasn't going to wait around for whatever was coming down this dreadful street. But Olivia wasn't herself, and her survival mechanisms had replaced all Daphne had ever known her to be.

'I'm sorry,' was all Olivia could muster. 'I can't. Sorry.'

She turned and walked quickly out the door, head down, and the front door thudded shut.

'Is that true?' asked Daphne of PC Foot, the colour now returning to his face.

'I think so,' he replied. 'I can't say. I'm sorry.' But he already had said. He jumped out of his skin when his radio emitted the once-calming tones of DI Bright, urgently wanting to be let in.

It wasn't just Bright who entered. A team of officers followed and filtered into the house as Bright joined Daphne in the lounge.

'Daphne,' he greeted her as he sat. Daphne was terrified having heard what she'd just been told, and now she'd been abandoned by her best friend. She just wanted to get the Hell out of there, but where would she go? Even police protection hadn't been good enough for Luke and his family. She was running out of places to go or hide.

But as the police went about their work checking the house was secure, who on earth was that in the lounge doorway in a grey shawl? Deanna Tamblyn, watching, standing completely still like the house had acquired a fourth mannequin, creepily staring in Daphne's own home.

'Why is she in here?' asked Daphne. Bright looked furious.

'Come on people!' he bellowed. 'Get her out of here.'

An officer walked her back out the front and the door thudded shut.

'What are we doing? You're losing it!' But it was Bright who was losing it.

A couple of officers entered the lounge and checked the windows, cable-tying them shut.

Bright half-composed himself and looked back to Daphne, searching for his old, calming persona but not managing to find it.

'Sorry about that. Listen, you're going to be safe tonight. Totally secure. No one is getting in here, okay? No one.'

'Here? I can't stay here. Take me into hiding, completely secret, like you did for Sara.' Daphne was desperate.

'That's not possible. I can't afford to risk anyone else. We will secure here for you.'

Daphne didn't know what that meant for Sara and Alfie. Had hiding not worked? Were they dead? But it wasn't just her friend's safety she was thinking about. If going into hiding with the police hadn't worked, then she had no hope. None at all. And now she was being told they weren't even going to do that.

'Is Sara okay?' she asked. 'Where is she?'

'I can't say anything right now.' The look on his face didn't bode well. But what came next was worse.

'They're dead,' came a voice from the doorway. It was PC Lyons, the big man with the beard. He looked beaten, losing it, struggling to hold onto any kind of normality. 'Just like the rest of them. Like our boys. My friends.' The big man cried, not attempting to wipe away any tears. 'Sir,' he said, looking at Bright, completely lost. 'I want to go home now.'

'Shut it Lyons!' was the snapped response from DI Bright, trying to get the job done. But Lyons snapped back louder.

'Fuck you, sir! Fuck you, and fuck this. I'm going home. Fuck this.' Lyons looked at Daphne through his tears, and stared with both fear and compassion. 'I'm sorry about your friends.' Lyons left and the front door creaked open and clicked closed, leaving Daphne on her seat, fighting the urge to cry but not quite managing it as her eyes started to fill.

'Is that true?' she asked. But Bright looked different again. Now he was the one with water filling his eyes. He looked straight at Daphne and mustered his strength.

'They're not dead yet.'

There was no way for Daphne to know what was true anymore. But wait. *Yet*? Why had he said that?

'Look. I've had to make some big decisions. But I think it's for the best. I've pulled in some more resources, bent a few rules. A lot of rules actually, all for your safety. You've got the whole force working for you now. You'll be safe. No one will get hurt tonight.' If only he looked like he believed it.

PC Joanne Bach, the friendly officer who'd first seen the scary painting, entered and addressed Bright.

'Sir, Nail needs to go home.'

'What's wrong with Nail?' asked Bright, though Daphne could tell he already knew the answer.

'You know, sir,' said Bach. 'Everyone's pretty keen to get out of here. It's getting dark.'

'Get out of here?' asked Daphne. 'You're not leaving me?' She looked at Andrew, who stood up.

86

'You'll be okay,' said Casper as he turned white as a ghost and followed Bach out the lounge door.

'You'll be secure,' said Bright. 'Totally safe. No one is getting in.'

'Is Andrew staying?' she asked.

Bright just looked at her as if he really wanted to say yes, but he was definitely saying no.

'Anyone? That lady?' Asked Daphne.

Bright's look didn't budge. Police walked past the lounge door one by one, all leaving the house. Leaving Daphne alone. Bright stood up.

'Right,' he shouted. 'Everybody out!'

Police officers flocked through the house and into the outside air as Bright walked to the lounge door, watching the last of them leave. He shouted one last time.

'Anyone else?' When no one answered, he spoke into his radio. 'House clearing now.' He turned to Daphne one last time with a scared but sorry look on his face, as if he was too guilty for any final words, and just stood, silently. Perhaps a useless apology would eventually come. But instead, the emotion drained from his face, and he said something that was certainly no apology.

'I'm glad your mother is dead,' he said, very matter-of-factly. As a creepy smile grew, his face changed in the most unnatural way, the eyes somehow sinking closer together and deeper into the skull. Then, from within those eyes, a sinister glow appeared that looked horribly like the eyes in the photograph. The room whiffed of rotting death as a new but familiar voice came out, guttural and creepy, exactly like something from her night terrors.

'You. Will. Burn.'

Then he turned, marched out at pace, and the front door thudded shut.

CHAPTER NINE

Daphne was desperate to be with other humans and not be left alone, but waited for the horribly weird DI Bright to get well clear before she went outside. The front door was closed and now, for some reason, was stuck shut. That's when the banging started.

Banging, all around. Right outside the front door, at the sides of the house and at the back. She had to get out. It was impossible. The door just wouldn't budge.

The bangs continued. Hammer blows. Then the whizzing buzz and rattle of an electric screwdriver. She was being barricaded in. Blocked. No one was getting in, but no one was getting out.

She ran back through the house to the kitchen but could hear the same thing happening. She grabbed and dropped the huge iron bar which clanged loudly on the floor, and yanked hard at the door, but it was never going to open. Planks of wood were being thrown up against the windows and all sorts of tools made a horrible cacophony of industrial sounds. Motors, bangs and rattles. She was being trapped. There was no escape.

The lounge window was already almost entirely boarded up, but there was a small gap between the planks and Daphne ran over to peer through and see what was going on and shout for help. There were ladders and machines outside hoisting people up on ropes, blocking up the upstairs windows. She barely noticed the two watching women across the road, Morwenna Rowe and Gugwana. They were the least of her worries.

The house was darkening, losing all of its natural light. All exit points were blocked. This wasn't a quick job to board up the windows. This went on and on. This was a serious job. No one was getting in. That, logically, should have made Daphne feel safer. Except it didn't. She was trapped, and if that wasn't bad enough, she'd seen all sorts of evidence that there was something already inside the house. The eyes that stalked her in the photograph. Whatever spoke to her in the night. Whatever broke the photo frame and moved it into the bathroom through the locked door. Whatever did that wasn't going to be stopped by wood and metal. Whatever did that was not of this world. Whatever did that was already inside the house. And Daphne was trapped inside with it.

Her phone! She still had a way to call for help. Her trembling fingers hit 999, but the voice that answered was no operator, nor human. It was a voice from her terrors.

'It's time to burn, Daphne,' it said, slowly, 'and burn you will,' before her phone got so hot it painfully singed her hand as she dropped it on the floor, the screen cracking and turning to darkness. She ran to her mother's old rotary dial and held it to her ear. She hadn't even dialled when the voice spoke. 'Burn.'

She ran to the front window, trying to get a glimpse of something, anyone who might save her. But there was nothing to see. Just wood against glass.

The noises outside stopped. The last of the banging slowed and came to an end. It was hard to hear what was going on outside, but it sounded like vehicles leaving. The rumble of vans disappeared into the distance. The last noises outside finally stopped, and there was silence.

Nothing.

Nothing but the sound of Daphne's heavy breathing that was about to turn to sobbing. But before the first cry came, something jolted her back into survival mode. One more noise. One that Daphne did not want to hear. One that made her as petrified as last night's terror-dream. A noise that was *inside the house*. Upstairs. Footsteps. Creeping quietly along the hallway.

Daphne ran back into the kitchen and picked up a big old knife that lay on the side. A knife that never blunted. Whatever it was, she was ready to defend herself. The police had panicked and run, and locked her in with the killer, whether that was human or otherwise. Now the killer was walking down the stairs in the dark, leaving Daphne to protect herself with a knife she'd only ever used to cut vegetables or something that was already dead.

The second step creaked its familiar creak.

A dark figure arrived at the bottom of the stairs and rounded the corner towards the kitchen. It was a man. Better than the alternative. At least a man could be stabbed. Was this the man with the camera? He looked a similar size. She'd gone for him once and survived, and now she had a knife. She could do this. She prepared herself to stab and stab hard, hiding just around the doorway in the kitchen shadows as the man-shaped figure moved slowly closer and closer.

Just three steps away now. Daphne gripped the knife harder, ready to strike. Two steps. Daphne breathed as quietly as she could, not even noticing her heart going crazy as she prepared to stab with all of her might.

One step into the kitchen and Daphne drove that knife with more strength than she'd ever used for anything in her whole life, right into the intruder's gut.

Andrew Foot jumped back in shock, pale as milk as the knife bounced off his stab vest and clattered across the hard kitchen floor.

Foot! Was it him? Is he the murderer? Daphne didn't know what to think as Foot looked at her, and then the knife on the floor next to the old bucket of water, composing himself.

'It's me. It's okay, it's me,' said Andrew, giving Daphne the biggest sense of relief she'd felt in her whole lifetime, though with a little scepticism remaining.

'How did you get in? Is there a way out up there?'

'No,' he replied. 'I hid when the order out was given. I never thought they'd actually do this. They shouldn't be leaving you alone.'

'They've trapped me.'

'They shouldn't have done that. Panic and desperation is what did that. But don't worry, I'm here too.'

Daphne didn't feel much safer.

'I've got something for you. Here.' Andrew passed Daphne a can of police-issue pepper spray as the colour returned to his face. 'Just to make you feel a little safer. Just point and spray, right in the face. That'll stop most people. But I'm sure you won't need it.'

'And if I do?' asked Daphne.

'You spray, and I'll make an arrest,' giggled Andrew nervously, growing a little paler again.

'So what now? I stabbed you. Are you okay?' asked Daphne.

Foot patted his hard, stiff stab vest. 'How about we sit down and put the telly on and pretend there's nothing wrong, shall we? If you knew what they'd just done you'd know it would take an army of tanks to get in here, really. Promise.'

'You got in,' said Daphne, not in any way convinced.

'They'll catch him, honestly. The guys are good. Now get that kettle on.'

Daphne didn't believe it, nor did she one hundred percent trust Andrew. She'd been warned by Deanna Tamblyn if nothing else, and if this six-foot man wanted to try anything, she'd be all alone.

'What about the man in the suit?' asked Daphne. He did this, he's...' but Daphne didn't want to say what she'd seen. No one would believe such a story, and she didn't want the uniformed officer to think she was crazy, or perhaps worse, a liar.

'He's a professional. I don't agree with this decision, but if he thinks it's for the best then it's to keep you safe. He's been in the job a long time.'

Daphne still didn't know what to say. She knew what she saw and heard.

Andrew switched on the TV and turned the channel away from the news, silencing Angela Shipman reporting on the murder, something that now appeared to be her full time job. This time she hadn't been outside on the street, but in the safety of a studio.

'Are we going to be okay?' asked Daphne, hoping for an honest answer. Surely Andrew knew something?

'Honestly,' said Andrew, pulling out a small packet of biscuits from his pocket, 'I really think this is a case of mass hysteria.'

'Not real?' asked Daphne. 'But there have been murders.'

'Yes, but those were all isolated to those three houses. Once the first one happened, I think people panicked, argued, maybe attacked each other. That's set off panic on the news, in the police, and now everything's just a bit crazy. The murderer right now will be hiding somewhere, wondering why he did something so stupid. And if he's hiding from us, he's not going to be coming anywhere near this place.'

'So it's just panic? But I've seen strange things too,' said Daphne, finally feeling a little hope. She knew a little about mass hysteria from the psychology videos on the internet. She'd sought them out to try to help herself feel better, but ended up going down all sorts of rabbit holes.

'Have you not heard of War of the Worlds?' asked Andrew.

'The film?'

'No,' smiled Andrew. 'It was a radio thing in the nineteen thirties. Same story as the film, but people heard it and thought it was a news report.'

Daphne smiled for the first time in a while.

'People panicked, got in their cars and sped away from the attackers from another world. It was crazy.'

'Mass hysteria?'

'Mass hysteria. And the Salem witch trials. Those poor women. It had the whole town panicking and killing each other. I'm sure that's what's going on here.'

'So how does this end?' asked Daphne. Amateur videos only explain so much.

'Well, the first thing is we don't join in the panic. And then it dies down and goes away. You're good Daphne, you're safe.'

Daphne felt a little safer and clung onto that hope. It was starting to make sense. There were a couple of strange ladies on this road, and a senile old woman doing very odd things. A mass murder at number ten had sparked off the hysteria, making them behave even more weirdly. The media enhanced the panic. Her own history of night terrors had come back and made a few things feel very real. The police, being humans too, had bought into the mass hysteria. The photo? Doctored. Timothy? A mad religious man who'd left America because he was nuts and no one there would listen. The photo in the bathroom? If Deanna Tamblyn had got in once, she could have got in before, and picking a bathroom lock can't have been that hard. DI Bright? Daphne was buying into the mass hysteria now too. Maybe he'd said 'I'm *sad* your mother is dead.'

It was all explainable. All of it. For the first time, Daphne relaxed just a little, and breathed a little easier. *Sad* and *glad*. She hadn't thought of that one before.

The longer the evening went on, the more normal things felt. Obviously not *that* normal, she was blocked in her own home with a police officer she barely knew. But things were making sense. It was just a psychological thing. No one could get in anyway. Eventually, she almost felt safe. And then she felt something she hadn't felt for days. Hungry.

She felt a little less safe as she walked alone into the kitchen, but that subsided as she cooked up some noodles without anything even slightly weird going on. She carried the plates of food to the lounge and they ate as a low-quality late-night film started. It looked terrible, but what else was there to do? A boring night would be so very welcome.

Not five minutes into the film, Andrew's attention had been completely taken by the TV. The bad movie was now showing a scene where the lead couple were getting passionate. Andrew was wrapped up in it, leaving Daphne feeling more than a little awkward. It might as well have been soft porn, and why Andrew, the one sat with the remote, hadn't turned it over she didn't know. Instead, he looked at her and smiled, then back to the screen, slurping his noodles into his mouth a little weirdly. The next time he looked at her, she was sure he looked her up and down. All of Daphne's feelings of safety disappeared. She was trapped with a strange man, policeman or not, watching almost-porn in her lounge, him clearly getting a little too excited and looking at her in places he wasn't welcome to look. Her thoughts returned to Deanna Tamblyn's warning, and then he spoke. She went extra quiet, doing her best with her body language to make herself look invisible.

'Need some tissue?' he asked, grinning then looking back at the TV's cheesy steamy scene. What a disgusting thing to say. Andrew looked at her knee again, making her feel more uncomfortable and now truly unsafe. 'Daphne,' he said firmly, looking at her knee. She looked down. She'd made a right mess of her dinner, and a big splodge of noodle and tomato was all over her knee. 'You need some tissue,' he said again. Daphne had never felt so relieved, and a little stupid, though he definitely ate his noodles weirdly. *Who slurps like that in someone else's home, seriously?*

And then the lights went out.

CHAPTER TEN

In the flickering light of the now irrelevant television sex scene, Andrew slowly stood, switching on his torch. He scanned the room quickly, but found nothing strange, weird or remotely creepy aside from the three mannequins, standing still in a row.

'Power cut?' asked Andrew.

'The telly's still on,' replied Daphne, a second before it switched off.

'You did that, right?' asked Andrew, his focus on the doorway as the shadows moved behind it as happens in the pitch dark in a moving torchlight.

'No.'

The remote lay out of reach on the table.

The only light in the whole house now was Andrew's torch. Not even the light of the moon or old streetlamps, kept out by the police barricades in the windows.

Andrew brought his torchlight back into the lounge, checking for anything that didn't seem right. One of the mannequins gently swayed. Its shadow ballooned behind as Andrew stepped closer to it.

'Don't panic,' he said. 'Remember what happens if we panic. This isn't War of the Worlds.'

'But what if there *is* a war coming?' asked Daphne, wondering if the police might know more than her about what Timothy had said, probing for a telling response.

'What?' replied Andrew, confused, as a second mannequin shadow rocked slowly. 'We should go somewhere brighter. Do you have any battery lights?'

'I have candles in my room.' Daphne got a nod from Andrew to follow him through the dark.

The creep up the stairs was slow, up over the second step's creak, with Andrew scouring up ahead with his light. Daphne closed the bedroom door behind them, and Andrew followed her with the beam so she could find her candles. She took them out and placed all three on the same black candlestick she'd brought back from Olivia's place. How she would have dearly loved to be there now.

Noticing the door was now open, she walked over and closed it, checking it was secure this time, then lit the candles. It was bright enough for Andrew to turn off his torch, just.

'What time are they letting us out?' asked Daphne.

'Sunrise, about six or seven. It's harder to panic in the sunlight, I guess.'

'What time is it now?' asked Daphne, wondering how long it would be until they got released.

'Half nine.'

'The candles won't last.'

'Then we'll sleep in the dark, like normal. No one can get in here,' said Andrew, closing the door.

Why did the door keep opening? That wasn't normal. Daphne pushed her desk across it.

'Really,' continued Andrew. 'No one can get in. We don't need to hide up here.'

In the candlelight which made all the shadows in the room dance, Daphne saw her painting now back up on the easel. She hadn't put it there. She'd dropped that horrible thing face down on the floor. The police who'd checked and secured the building shouldn't have touched that, she thought, creeped out by the horrible painted creature, reminding her of that photograph. It gave her the shivers, literally, and Andrew noticed her shaking.

'No one can get in here Daphne. I promise. You're safe in here with me.'

'Someone did,' said Daphne, standing still. She'd heard the stair creak, and now footsteps were getting closer. This wasn't panic or hysteria or one of her nightmares. Andrew could hear them too, and pulled out his baton. They were close now, at the top of the stairs. Daphne instinctively grabbed the only possible weapon she could find, a super-sharp pencil from her easel.

'Spray can,' whispered Andrew as he flicked and extended his baton, ready. Daphne took the pepper spray from her belt. The steps got even closer, moving slowly. Right up outside the bedroom door, where they stopped.

Andrew shuffled closer to the door, baton raised high, listening intently. But there was nothing. Nothing but silence.

Nothing but two terrified humans standing in the flickering candlelight, knowing there was an intruder who was likely a mass killer, but not knowing who, or what, it was. And he, or it, was right outside the door, silent.

Until the door-tapping started.

Tap, tap, tap. Silence again.

Tap, tap, tap.

'Police. Identify yourself,' called Andrew, his voice cracking up as his face faded to a pale white. The tapping got firmer. Slower.

Tap.

Tap.

Tap.

And then the candles went out, the room falling into complete darkness. Daphne could see nothing. Nothing at all. Until Andrew fumbled with and then switched on his torch.

The desk was back in its original place. The door was open. A mannequin stood right in front of Andrew, making him jump back in shock as his torchlight picked out its creepy cracked head, causing a huge shadow to move across the wall. Daphne screamed like she'd never screamed before as all the lights in the house flickered.

Andrew ran through the door, Daphne following, down the stairs, as quick as they could, but at the bottom, Andrew froze, stopping Daphne in her tracks. She looked back over her shoulder. Nothing was there. Nothing following them. Nothing but the cold breeze which shouldn't have been there.

But Andrew was looking a different way. One of the lights in the house had come back on. Andrew directed Daphne's eyes to the bottom of the door of the old storeroom, where a slither of light came through under the gap. Moving across that slither of light, was a shadow. Something was in there, moving.

'Spray if you have to,' whispered Andrew, readying his baton. 'Use all of it.'

Whoever the intruder was, he was in that room. Between baton and spray, he was going down.

Andrew passed his torch to Daphne, gesturing to shine it at the door, refusing to be blinded by darkness again. He raised his baton, ready to strike and strike hard.

Andrew yanked the door open and jumped inside, ready for combat. But there was no one in there. Just an empty room with the light on. Nothing unusual at all. But behind Daphne, the lounge door slowly creaked open.

She swung her torch around, but the door was now still.

'The light's on,' whispered Andrew. 'The electric's back. Turn on the lounge lights.'

They walked quietly, pointing the torch in through the lounge door. Nothing unusual. Nothing but two mannequins, side by side, looking creepy in the torchlight.

Daphne reached around the corner, feeling for the familiar light switches. As she flicked them and the lights came on, she screamed.

Andrew jumped in, ready to strike, but saw no one in the empty room.

'Something touched my arm,' she said, shaking, as Andrew moved quickly around, checking any possible hiding places, ready for a fight. But there was no one there. Nothing.

'My arm's wet,' said Daphne, reminded of her night terror when she felt her face being licked by something invisible.

'It's sweat,' replied Andrew.

But it wasn't sweat. It was too thick and sticky for that, and the terrible smell had returned.

'And why,' Daphne asked, 'were the lights switched off if it was a power cut?'

Andrew was starting to panic, doing his best to rationalise, trying anything to keep his fear away.

'It's sweat,' he said again. 'Mass hysteria. That's why the confusion. It's all in our heads.'

'But it's not, is it?' Daphne refused to deny reality anymore. Either she was as far gone as poor old Gugwana, or they were in genuine danger, being hunted by something incredibly clever and dark.

'Nothing is happening!' shouted Andrew, losing the plot. The lights dimmed, and Andrew burst into tears, looking like a small boy version of himself, refusing to believe the truth. 'Nothing!'

Now, imagine a rope had been tied around Andrew's ankles and his feet yanked hard from under him, his flailing body dragged out of the room and speedily across the carpet. That's exactly what it looked like to Daphne. Except there was no rope. Whatever had dragged him was invisible, and fast, and Andrew was gone. Daphne looked around the doorway down the hall where she saw him lying on the kitchen floor fighting and swinging his baton for just a second or two until the kitchen door slammed shut. And then there was silence. Nothing. Nothing but Daphne, all alone. Nothing until the final scream of a terrified policeman who'd tried his best.

Daphne darted back into the lounge and shut the door. She slid the sofa in front of it, then pulled down the bookshelf on top of it, desperately trying to block the door, but somehow knowing it was pointless. She stepped back into the room, looking for something, anything, to help her escape this mess. Her worst nightmares, her childhood night terrors, were all coming true. Was this just another terror? They'd always felt real but this time it felt different. This one *was* real. There was nothing else to block the door with, and really, she knew that wouldn't help anyway. She was beaten, and no one was there to help her. If they had been, they wouldn't have been able to help anyway. It was over. This was how it would all end, with her alone in the house, scared, and completely helpless, living out her worst childhood nightmares for real. But there was one thing in that room that could give her some comfort in her final moments, so she knelt down by the big cardboard box labelled 'Mum,' and hugged it.

'I need you, Mum,' she cried. 'I really need you right now.' And the lights went off.

Complete darkness. She could see nothing. Nor hear anything. Nothing at all.

Nothing but a faint single ray of light piercing the barricades in the window.

Nothing but the back of the mannequin it landed on, completely still.

Nothing else at all.

Nothing but the faint sound of footsteps growing closer, from the kitchen towards the lounge door.

Closer. It had arrived.

Tap, tap, tap.

Daphne scoured the room with the torch. There was nothing unusual, apart from the sofa across the door and the bookshelf pulled on top of it, with old leather-bound books and manuals lying all around.

Tap, tap, tap.

This was it. She had nothing to fight with, whatever this was, and now it was coming for her. And then she saw movement. Movement coming under the door. A whiff of smoke, getting thicker, wafting in. And the smell. It smelled of burning steak. And then the smoke alarm went off.

A fire. The house was on fire, and she had nowhere to go. She ran over to the windows and smashed at them with her fists and elbows. But the windows were strong. Bullet-proof, perhaps. She knew she had no chance. Still, she smashed and smashed at them, hoping someone might hear and help. But no one came. No one could see nor hear her, and she knew it.

Smoke piled under the door. She knew she had a choice to make. Die in a fire like the whispering voices had said, sizzle and char on the kitchen floor like her teenaged nightmares had foretold, burn as DI Bright had so gleefully told her to. Or, open the lounge door and fight the fire. Whatever it was in the house, maybe that would take her first and give her a more painless end than burning to death like the Salem witches. She had to get to the kitchen for water, and hope it was enough. She hooked the pepper spray back over her belt and pulled the heavy wooden bookshelf off the sofa, kicked the books out the way across the floor, and pulled away the sofa. There was now just a thin wooden door between her and whatever it was, but she had no choice. She wasn't going to burn to death. She wasn't going to let those old night terrors play out for real.

She opened the door and ran out into the smoke, but instead of running to the kitchen, instinct took her to the front door, where she grabbed the handle and pulled and yanked as hard as she could, screaming to be let out. But no one came. There was no help anywhere. Nothing. And the smoke was getting thicker.

She ran through to the kitchen, wrapping her clothes around her mouth and nose, to the source of the smoke. It wasn't a house fire at all. It was the old black cooker, bellowing out smoke, turned up as high as the huge dials would allow, a huge flame glowing brightly through the glass. She switched it off, burning her hand painfully as she did. And then she saw.

Something was inside, burning.

Whatever it was smelled rancid, making her almost vomit. Looking through the glass front, she saw it. Andrew Foot's head, charred black and burning, his eyes still in the sockets as if staring, but bubbling and bulging, ready to pop in the heat. She nearly jumped a foot in the air when the toaster sprung up, fountaining blistered severed fingers over the sides.

'Stop it!' she screamed at whatever it was doing this. If she was going to die, she might as well take up the anger's invitation and yell and scream back at whatever was going to kill her. She'd throw a fist too if given a chance.

A cheese grater flew through the smoke, hitting her right in the face, cutting the end of her nose so badly it would scar if only she had that kind of time left. Then the wooden rolling pin, which hurt, but honestly, she didn't care. She was as angry as she was scared, but more than that, beaten and with nothing to lose. The thick wooden chopping board hit her hard. She scrambled back, looking for what might be coming next. But as she did, she tripped and knocked over the bucket of water, still on the floor after the fire outside. The water spread across the kitchen floor as Daphne stumbled back and fell, landing on her backside against the wall, her feet on the wet floor out in front of her.

As the water flowed across the kitchen floor, it parted around two invisible feet, facing right at her. The water flowed in to fill where one invisible foot was, then another foot imprint appeared in the water in front of the other with a little splash. This was it. She could lie there and die, fight, or get up and run.

She ran. Back towards the front door, where she pulled and yanked and screamed and shouted but no one came. She was beaten, once and for all. This was the end. She turned and sank down against the door, looking back down the corridor towards the kitchen, where wet footprints were appearing on the carpet, slowly, one by one, heading in her direction. And then they charged. Daphne threw up her hands and turned her head, squeezing her eyes shut, bracing herself for impact, and death, hearing the thudding of feet hurtling at her through the hallway. But the impact never came. Instead, the thuds stopped not an inch away. She opened her eyes. The wet footprints were right in front of her. Her nose began to bend back a bit, as if being pushed by an invisible finger.

Because it was.

Pulling the pepper spray from her belt, she tried her last chance, and sprayed right in front of her, up above the footprints. The spray clung to an invisible face, sticking to and revealing the outline of something that almost looked like a wild dog, or lizard, or something in between. She sprayed and sprayed as the layer of chemical liquid on the invisible creature got thicker, making the details of its face clear, while the back of its body disappeared back into nothingness. This was no dog or lizard, nor really anything like either. She didn't stop spraying until the can ran out. She pulled the trigger again and again, but nothing more came. It was over. The eyelids made of chemical spray slowly parted sideways, revealing two holes right through the face. The eyes slowly revealed themselves through those holes, just as they had looked in that photograph. In her night terrors. The face moved closer to hers. Slowly, inching closer, until it was barely a hair away.

Daphne closed her eyes, refusing to see what was about to happen, braced herself for the pain, and waited for her life to end.

And there it was again, that horrible feeling of being slowly licked from her chin to her hairline. And the smell.

That rancid smell of death.

***

They say when you're about to die, your whole life flashes through your mind. This was true for Daphne, except it wasn't a cartoonish set of pictures running chronologically from her childhood of all her important moments. It was her whole life as it was now. All her thinking patterns and beliefs. All the bullshit she told herself about herself and the world to maintain her sense of identity and protect her. Everything that was important to her and wasn't. And she saw it all with crystal clarity and with an honesty she'd never felt before.

She'd been given a choice right at that moment. She could crack and break, and completely dissociate from reality, like poor old Gugwana had. Pretend she was invisible and lie back and let her own sanity leave her head, rendering the death of her physical body pretty painless. Reality would happen and bring her physical demise, but she'd be too far gone to care. Or she could go the other way, and stare reality in the face, demons or no demons. She chose reality in its realist form, and in her mind, saw everything.

She saw herself at college, going through the motions of fashion design not because she enjoyed it, but because she wanted to be part of that world, and she wanted other girls to see her being part of that world, and to think she was special. Maybe she wouldn't be so invisible then.

She saw her friendship with Olivia, not because she truly liked her, but because she wanted to be just like her, the magnetic girl who *everyone* noticed.

She saw how she truly felt about Sara, and though she'd been trying desperately to become more like Olivia, Sara was the one she saw deep down as a true shining light, somehow more a sister than a friend.

She saw her unusual attack on the angry reporter with the tomato head, and saw that it wasn't just out of fear, it was because he reminded her of an old school history teacher who'd bullied her until she cried, bringing about the very moment she'd learned that not to be seen was to be safe.

She saw her date with Luke at fourteen and saw that she didn't refuse a second date because he was too nice, but because of how he looked at her, really seeing her, and that made her uncomfortable. She'd made other excuses ever since.

She saw her aversion to all things religious and supernatural, and saw that it wasn't because she thought it was silly, but because she knew if it was true, then she was somehow a part of it, and that was far too much for a young mind to accept. If the world, universe and any other realms are all connected, then everyone is part of it, and so is she, connected to all like her, except she knew she was really somehow different. She'd been so anti-supernatural because deep down, she'd been drawn to it, a part of it, and didn't want that to be true. She didn't want power like that. She was just a young girl. And as she saw all that so clearly, it felt like Gugwana had reached out and held her hand and guided her through.

What a beautiful person Gugwana really was, and how sad it was to see her decline. Though from a different continent and two generations apart, and though Daphne didn't even know her surname, Gugwana felt like a true sister.

But most of all, she saw how she judged herself as somehow insufficient for the world. Not good enough. All those times she seemed so invisible, she'd brought it on herself quite deliberately, if subconsciously. If others really saw her, they'd see her that way too. Not worthy. Useless. Better to not be seen at all. So she became socially invisible, and got good at it. That's why on the surface she'd been so desperate to be like Olivia, a girl who everyone saw as perfect.

She saw it all, so clearly. She was no longer making herself invisible to herself, at least. And she accepted it.

And so it seems that that's what is meant by seeing your whole life flash before your eyes. There's no greatest hits show at the end, just a clear picture of how one's entire life really is. The whole thing had taken seconds, but felt like an eternity, each new thought pattern and emotion now deeply processed, her new beliefs about herself ingrained, new neural pathways formed and forged. In those moments before death, she truly saw and knew herself right to her core. And, surprisingly, she quite liked what she saw. If only she had time left to enjoy being that woman before it was all taken from her by the stinking demon a few inches from her face.

She opened her eyes, ready to face her fate, and it was terrifying.

The creature's face was breathing on her with a smell so strong it masked even that of the pepper spray. Then, for no obvious reason, it looked up, then turned. Wet footprints appeared again, this time thudding down the hallway in the other direction. Daphne was left in the doorway on the floor next to the destroyed doorbell box and batteries still strewn across the floor, somehow still breathing, terrified but with a whole new way of seeing her world, as if that still mattered.

Where had the creature gone? Why had it gone? Daphne had no idea. She'd readied herself for the end, but it hadn't come. She'd expected to feel nothing by now but instead felt the excruciating sting in her eyes of the pepper spray.

And then, on the floor in front of her, from the powerless and broken box and hanging snapped wires she'd so angrily smashed to pieces, the impossible happened one more time. The doorbell rang.

That damned doorbell.

CHAPTER ELEVEN

Ding dong.

The doorbell didn't scare her this time, even if was ringing impossibly.

'Come in,' she said out loud, almost laughing to herself. If she was going out now, she might as well go out with a smile.

When the letterbox flap opened, she thought it was over. The whole thing had been shut up with heavy machinery, and now the letterbox was opening. She was free!

Except she wasn't.

The door still wouldn't open. And now a hand was coming through the letterbox, feeling around with its old skin and long nails.

'Are you there, dear?' enquired a croaky voice from outside. Daphne kept as quiet as a mouse as the hand disappeared back outside. She looked through the spyhole, trying to see anything she could, but it was just black. Still boarded up. No way in and still no way out.

When she turned around, she jumped. In front of her, in the dark hallway, stood three women. Deanna Tamblyn. Gugwana. Morwenna Rowe with her shining red hair and old wooden broomstick in hand, a thick ornamental metal cap on the end of the handle.

'Did he get inside you, dear?' asked Deanna Tamblyn. 'He didn't get inside you, did he? You can't let him get inside you.'

'Oh she's fine, Deanna,' said Morwenna Rowe. 'Stop dallying.'

'Leave her be, sister,' said Gugwana, looking with her wonderful smile at her old friend Daphne, now all grown up.

'Well, she fusses,' argued back Morwenna.

'I fuss for a reason, Morwenna,' said Deanna.

'Fuss fuss fuss,' taunted Morwenna.

'Will somebody drop a house on her?' responded Deanna.

'Quiet, ladies, please,' asked Gugwana, looking like she had work to do.

It was all very odd. These ladies had appeared out of nowhere just as Daphne had resigned herself to death, and now here they were, bickering in her hallway like children.

'How did you get in? Is there a way out?'

Morwenna Rowe leaned in close to Daphne again, followed by Deanna, Daphne staying as silent as she was confused.

'Where did he go?'

'Yes where did he go, dear?'

'Deanna, will you get out of that poor girl's face,' said Morwenna Rowe, also still in Daphne's face.

'I'm just checking,' replied Deanna. 'Somebody here has to check.'

'Stop it now, both of you,' said Gugwana, glaring down the hallway towards the kitchen. Morwenna's neck twisted unnaturally around to face straight at Deanna.

'Yes, stop it Deanna,' croaked Morwenna.

'Stop!' shouted Deanna. There was finally silence. Deanna and Morwenna stood up straight together and turned, Deanna's neck straightening stiff.

When Gugwana chanted, her voice dealt only in sounds that Daphne's ears had yet to hear.

'Hear us now, from the dark,' joined Morwenna, almost musically.

'From the halls,' said Deanna, looking serious.

As Gugwana's chanting climaxed, Morwenna stood up tall and shouted.

'Trap this demon within these walls!' She stamped her broomstick handle hard on the floor to the sound of an almighty bang as all the lights in the house flashed bright before sinking gently back to darkness.

Then quiet. Nobody moved. Nothing.

Nothing but three magical older ladies and a teenaged woman who was no longer denying reality. The rumours of her childhood had been true. There were witches on

Hanging Hill Lane. A noose wasn't good enough to finish them off all those years ago, after all.

The witches walked down into the kitchen, following the damp footsteps on the carpet, as Daphne had another realisation.

Gugwana and Morwenna stood back-to-back in the centre of the kitchen, circling slowly and stiffly with unflattering wide stances. Deanna stood with Daphne, ready, her own personal witch bodyguard.

'What do you mean, get inside of me?' asked Daphne of Deanna. 'You're talking about possession, aren't you?'

'A demon, my dear, can easily possess a human,' Deanna replied, eyes scouring the kitchen. 'They're weak and have no morals.'

'It didn't get me,' replied Daphne, feeling a little proud but also insulted.

'They can get most, my dear, though some are immune. Sadly not that human so-called in charge of those so-called police, for one.'

That made sense. The eyes. The voice.

'Too weak,' said Morwenna.

'Too immoral,' said Gugwana, correcting her. 'We freed that poor man but an hour ago, but he won't be right for a while. He doesn't have it in him to recover with haste.'

'Too immoral,' said Morwenna.

'Too weak,' corrected Gugwana, Morwenna noticing too late that Gugwana was winding her up.

'But a witch,' continued Deanna, leaning in close to Daphne while her eyes still scanned the kitchen sideways as if looking out the side of her head, 'a demon will only manage to possess an inexperienced witch with a broken heart and a broken mind. And that, my dear, is why they are here now, breaking your mind.'

'Breaking my mind?' asked Daphne. They'd managed that, surely? She was beaten just a few minutes ago, accepting death. 'Why me? Why not one of you?'

'Your mother was a dear friend, dear. It broke all of our hearts when they took her, but no doubt broke yours most of all. It'll be why they did it. Sorry dear, not your fault.'

Daphne was now completely confused, but Deanna remained completely focused on the kitchen, the other two witches still slowly circling, back-to-back, broomstick raised ready.

'She kept you away from it all. Not your fault.' Deanna continued. 'But they knew that. They watch from the shadows. And so having broken your heart they only needed to break your mind, and they'd have got in you, my dear.'

'You'll frighten the poor girl!' snapped Morwenna, still circling and allowing only a split-second glance at Deanna with one eye before putting both eyes firmly back on the kitchen, scanning for signs of the invisible beast.

'A possessed witch,' continued Deanna, completely ignoring Morwenna.

'A night witch,' interrupted Gugwana before Deanna continued.

'Well, that would be a disaster. Especially with the war coming. What took you so long to let us in, dear?'

'As did dilly the mother, so does dally the daughter,' said Morwenna.

Daphne was trying to work out what on earth was going on, trying to understand what she'd just heard, and fit it into everything that had happened. But she couldn't. For that to be true, she'd have to be a witch, and she didn't want to be. And certainly not a night witch, whatever that was.

'What she's trying to say, my dear young witch,' said Morwenna, 'is would you like to join us in hunting this little demon that hides somewhere, bound within these walls?'

'Trapped,' said Gugwana with a smile which made the dark room a little more visible.

'Trapped but not yet caught, not yet found nor banished,' mumbled Morwenna.

'Stop!' shouted Gugwana. Everyone stopped. Gugwana had seen something. 'There's a head in the oven again.'

'Oh we can't have that,' said Deanna. 'That would make for trouble. Make that disappear someone will you.'

They all stopped, scanning the room, eyes jerking circles in perfectly still heads.

And then they started to speak again.

'It's not in here,' said Morwenna.

'The head?' asked Gugwana.

'The demon,' said Morwenna, 'Nor the head. I vanished that one. Body too.'

'Hiding,' said Gugwana.

'Nowhere to run, dear,' said Deanna to Daphne.

'Trapped,' smiled Gugwana.

'Why is it here?' asked Daphne, still confused.

'Oh my dear, you're as slow as your mother was,' said Deanna. Morwenna walked over to Daphne and leaned in close to her face again.

'They want to take your mind,' she said, 'your body, and your magic. To use it for reasons that do not bear thinking about, not even for one single thought.'

'A night witch,' interrupted Gugwana.

'But there is a war coming and we cannot lose, and you will not succumb. We will send it back,' continued Morwenna.

'So what do you say, dear?' said Deanna to Daphne, getting excited. 'Let's go hunt us some demon!'

'Oh Deanna,' said Morwenna. 'You do sound so ridiculous when you try to sound like the children.'

'The sentiment is the sentiment,' offered Gugwana, pulling a huge decorative knife from inside her colourful long jacket. The knife adornments were as richly coloured as her clothes. She noticed Daphne spot it, so smiled at her old friend. 'Sometimes, to be seen, you need a bit of colour,' she whispered.

And then they all stopped, listening. What was that sound? It came from the lounge. Morwenna Rowe twisted the richly patterned metal cap from the end of her broomstick handle and pulled it off, revealing the end to be shaved into a razor-sharp point. Gugwana readied her huge knife and stepped towards the hallway, quietly. The others followed, Deanna never leaving Daphne's side. As she left the kitchen, Daphne picked up a knife from the rack, one of the knives that had never blunted in all these years.

'That's not going to help you in here, dear,' said Deanna as they followed the others out.

'Then again...' said Gugwana with a wink.

Into the lounge they walked. First Gugwana, then Morwenna, and finally Daphne and Deanna. They moved slowly, quietly, ready.

'He's in here,' said Gugwana.

'Seal the door, Deanna,' said Morwenna. 'He must not flee. Come on, dilly dally.'

Deanna stood near the doorway, raised her hand, and the door flung itself shut.

'Reveal yourself, demon!' shouted Morwenna, gripping her pointed broomstick.

They all went quiet, and Gugwana began her chant.

'Invisible beast, show us your form.'

'Show us yourself, your eyes and your horns,' followed Morwenna.

'Very good Morwenna, that was a good one,' said Deanna, then turning to Daphne. 'You'd better go and stand over there, dear,' she said, gesturing to near the box of her mother's possessions, before joining the other two witches in the centre of the room. Gugwana continued.

'Invisible beast, it's time to reveal,'

'You can no longer hide,' said Deanna.

'No longer conceal,' said Morwenna, getting a sarcastic approving look from Deanna for her quick-witted rhyme.

'Reveal,' said Gugwana.

'Reveal,' said Deanna.

'Reveal,' said Morwenna, eyes jerking. And then all three.

'Reveal! Reveal! Reveal!' Daphne couldn't help but join.

'Reveal, reveal!'

And then it did.

Cowering in the corner was the beast from the photograph, its back no longer fading into nothing, but a full animal the size of a goose but no bird, mammal or reptile. The eyes were all too familiar to Daphne, who'd seen them too many times now. In the photograph, above her bed, the painting, right in front of her as she cowered at the front door. But now, it knew it was beaten.

'It's a small one,' said Morwenna.

'Just a young one,' said Gugwana.

'It's too small,' said Deanna, looking worried. 'Dispatch it, quick.'

'Into the ear, that's the spot,' said Gugwana.

'I know, woman, stop bothering me with things I learned long ago,' Morwenna snapped back, as Gugwana gave Daphne another little wink.

'Well hurry on with it then, it is you who dallies,' said Deanna, provoking a stern look back.

'Be banished, demon!' shouted Morwenna, 'Be gone, spawn!'

'The spell needs to end on a rhyme,' pointed out Deanna. 'That's barely an acquaintance of a good rhyme.'

'Well it's good enough for the magic,' snapped back Morwenna. 'Have a better one? No? Well then,' she said as she raised her spiked broomstick high in a huff.

It sounded like a shriek from Hell as Morwenna drove the spiked handle into the beast, right through its ear, and the beast disappeared back into nothingness.

'Is it dead?' asked Daphne.

'Don't be silly, they don't die, dear,' said Deanna.

'Is it gone?' asked Daphne, thinking that this whole nightmare might finally be over.

But the witches looked worried, scouring the room with their jerky eyes, ready for a fight.

'If that was a young one,' said Morwenna, 'then the mother is here.'

'There is only one mother I know of right now,' said Gugwana.

'That's what worries me,' said Deanna, followed by a silence that hadn't been heard since they'd arrived. But the stillness didn't last long.

The lounge door flew open and off its hinges, right across the room straight into Gugwana, knocking her flat on the floor. The hair of the witches, including Daphne, blew around in wind that was impossible to be there.

'Reveal yourself, demon!' shouted Morwenna.

'She's hardly going to do that, is she dear?' said Deanna.

Morwenna stabbed into the darkness, hoping she might hit something, as Gugwana climbed to her feet, holding her knife, but was flung back down to the floor by something invisible and hugely strong. Morwenna took the chance to stab at where the beast must have been, right above Gugwana, but instead her broomstick was yanked from her hands, the spike snapped off and fired straight back at her, piercing her throat, and her broomstick thrown to the floor by the empty doorway. Morwenna Rowe slumped to the floor, dead. Gugwana got up again, but flew straight back into the wall, hard, and was banged against it time and time again. Deanna tried to fight back but was flung against the wall too. Bang! Bang! Bang against the wall, and Gugwana flopped down, a lifeless body in colourful clothes. Deanna sat on the floor, beaten, and looked to Daphne, cowering behind the box.

'Don't let her get inside you,' were the last words she said before she was picked up and snapped in two, her head removed and dropped on the floor. But Deanna hadn't given up.

'You'll have to do better than that, dear,' said Deanna's head to the invisible beast. Deanna's eyes looked to Daphne and to the broken broomstick on the floor, and then back to the beast, or where she thought it was, at least.

'Let me tell you a little tiny tale, beasty,' the head continued. 'But first, would you like to reveal yourself? It's a story about a pathetic little demon and how it got removed from this world by a broomstick I made myself, just for that job.' Deanna was buying time for Daphne, who ran out the lounge door, grabbing the broken broomstick from the floor as she went, then up the stairs as quickly and quietly as she could, stepping over that second stair.

'Goodbye for now, dear,' were the final words Deanna's head said before Daphne heard a loud crunch and bang, just as she pulled her bedroom door shut, broomstick in one hand and her mother's knife in the other.

As she crouched behind the bed, she started to sharpen the snapped end of the broomstick, just as she had done with all those pencils a thousand times before. A broom handle was a tougher job than a pencil, but that knife, in all those years, had always been sharp, and shavings quickly mounted on the floor. She knew there was little time. The beast would come for her next, and either kill her, or break her and take her.

She could hear the beast downstairs. It wasn't small footsteps like before. These were big, thumping stomps, moving slowly through the house down there. The new spike of the broom handle was starting to take shape as the stomps downstairs travelled into the kitchen.

Daphne didn't want to be a witch, but with all she'd just seen and heard, she was starting to accept it. She'd spent her whole life refusing the existence of the supernatural, and sometimes even mocked the ridiculousness of those who believed. Except they'd been right. She lived in the very place where witches would be hanged to death all those years ago. She didn't want to have any part of it, let alone have that kind of power. Except now, she *needed* that power. It was use it and have a chance of living, or not use it, and have a pretty big chance of dying, or even bringing Lord-knows what kind of darkness into the world. But to use that power, she would have to accept she had it, and that was a step she didn't want to take. As she looked at the sharp point of the broom handle, she knew she had no choice. She was a witch, and she was going to have to act like one.

The stomps stomped to the bottom of the stairs, slowly moving closer. The second stair creaked. This thing was invisible, and if the three old witches couldn't make it reveal itself, what chance did Daphne have? She had no idea how. So she turned to the thing that had got her out of trouble her whole life. *Sometimes, to be seen, you need a bit of colour.*

The stomps were now upstairs and sounded like they had gone into her mother's room. Daphne opened up her paint pots, pouring them quickly on the floor by the door. If this thing came in, she would see the footprints again, and have some idea where to stab. It was a long shot, but all she had. The picture on the easel now looked exactly like the small demon that had been cowering in the lounge, the child of the monster that now hunted her, and it looked terrifying. The stomps came closer, right outside her door.

Daphne wasn't ready. She hadn't yet worked out her plan. She had a weapon, and laid her paint trap, but she was still working things out. She wasn't ready to fight. Nor was she ready to accept that she was a witch. But ready or not, the time had arrived. She darted behind the bed, broomstick in one hand, her last full pot of paint in the other. If she had a chance, she could throw the paint and reveal the demon, just like her can of pepper spray had. It was the closest thing to a plan she had. Simple, and probably doomed to fail. But it was all there was. *If I'm going to be a witch, act like one*, she thought to herself, not having any idea how that meant she needed to act.

The door opened.

Daphne ducked down low behind the bed, with a slight view across the floor. She could see the carpet covered in paint by the door. Legs of the easel. Wood chippings from all the pencils she'd ever sharpened. And a footprint appearing in the paint by the door.

Then nothing. It was like the demon had stopped. Had it worked out her plan? Where was it now? Could it fly? That would really mess things up. But then she got lucky.

A second footprint appeared in the paint. Her position under the bed concealed her from the hunter and gave her a chance to strike first, as long as it didn't drop its head too low and see her. The invisible hunter took another step into the room. It stank.

Should she throw the paint over the bed like some kind of paint grenade? It would be a brave move, and reveal the demon to her, but also her to the demon. And then she'd lose. No, she had to stay hidden. A red-paint footprint appeared another step into the room. It was getting closer. Then another.

What could she do? Jump out and attack, trying to surprise it? Wait and hide until it found her? Another step closer it came. She had to decide quick. If she waited until she was found, she would die. But then something unexpected happened. As it reached the legs of the easel, it stopped. A paint footprint appeared facing the easel legs by the years of childhood shavings. Then another. It took Daphne a few seconds to realise. It was looking at the picture. The painting of the hunter's own child.

If ever there was an opportunity, it was now. If the demon mother's legs were pointing that way, and she was looking at the picture, then she surely couldn't be looking anywhere else, and Daphne would know exactly where the hunter was. She had a shot. Only one, but it was a shot.

As she silently raised her head above the bed and looked, she saw something she wasn't expecting. The invisible mother's face was partly revealed, face to face with the picture. But the painting was no longer just a painting. It was now coming out in three dimensions, or more likely four, being somehow sucked out of the canvas and into the room. It was like she was drawing her child out from within the painting and back into the human world, and within seconds, Daphne would be fighting not one demon, but two. But this was her shot. It was partially visible, a few feet away from her, and distracted. It was do, now, or die.

The supernatural, Daphne now knew all too well, was real. She was no longer denying reality. She was a witch and she would behave like one, and it seemed that meant slaying demons. She plunged that broomstick into the distracted demon's side, ripping it away from the picture which shrank back to two dimensions on the canvas as the mother crashed down on its side, covering itself in paint, the broomstick sticking straight up. She'd hurt it, but it was still moving. And then Daphne saw what she didn't want to see: the mother started to stand, covered in paint on one side, the broomstick sticking out the other. It turned to face her, and Daphne had nothing.

Nothing but fear.

Nothing but the knowledge of who she was, and what she had to do. She just didn't know how to do it. The creature stepped towards her, and she didn't budge.

Daphne hadn't had any training in the ways of the witch, so she tried the only thing she'd seen them do.

'Reveal yourself, demon!' she screamed at it. 'Reveal yourself!' But nothing happened. It just stayed still, staring at her with eyes that were beginning to glow. And then it stepped forward, flinging her to the ground with an invisible hand. The demon plucked the broomstick out of itself and smacked Daphne with it hard. Once, twice, three times as she lay on the floor, unable to defend herself or get up, and only managing to avoid being killed by the point she'd carved herself by rolling under the bed just before the next strike came. She rolled quickly under to the other side of the bed next to the open pot of paint, ready but now of no use at all.

Except it was. Daphne wasn't beaten. She wouldn't crack. She wouldn't let it break her mind or take her body. She didn't have any kind of command of magic to fight with, and three experienced witches had already tried magic and suffered horrible ends. But she did have something else. An invitation, and instructions from her mother about how to use it.

Anger.

When anger comes with instructions and quick wits, it's deadly. To suppress it, to attempt the quietness of invisibility as she always had, would be the end of her. She grabbed the invitation with both hands, and flung that paint as hard as she could. Not at the mother, but at the painting, hitting the picture of the demon young right in the face, covering it in a spray of thick white paint. The mother screamed a deafening, screeching roar, but didn't go for revenge. Instead, it dropped the broomstick and walked over to the painting, and licked it. Then again. And again. She was cleaning off the white paint from her child, either from some motherly animal instinct or because the messy white covering would stop her from bringing it back from whatever dimension it had been banished to. But she didn't get a chance. Daphne thrust the broomstick point in again, and again, as the mother fell back, partly revealing her true form, a horrifying beast that was ten times the size of the child and had two great wings coming out of its scaley back.

Again and again, in went the spiked broomstick, but the mother would not die.

'Die!' Daphne shouted. 'Die, die!' as the broomstick plunged in and out, leaving the beast flailing on the floor.

But then, replaying in her mind, which was now completely on her side, Daphne heard the voice of Deanna Tamblyn. What had she said? *Don't be silly, they don't die, dear.* And that's when she remembered Morwenna Rowe, and how she'd done it. The demon's face revealed fully, horned, with three tongues, and spoke with a familiar voice from the terrors, taking advantage of Daphne's pause as it lay wounded on the floor but with wounds fast healing, quickly regaining its strength.

'You're nothing, you are a stupid, pointless little girl. Weak like a human. Unworthy, like a human.' But Daphne had worked it out.

'Be banished, demon!' she shouted as she raised her broomstick high with one hand, pushing her hair out of her face with the other. 'I'm a witch, bitch!' She brought that broomstick spike down as hard as she could, piercing the demon's ear and right through the head, the sharp end breaking off on the floorboards below as the lights flashed bright and the walls of the house echoed the final scream from the mother beast. And then there was silence. The demon was no longer there. There was nothing left of it. Nothing at all.

Nothing but a young witch, having beaten her first demon.

Nothing but a painted picture of a cat with beautiful big blue eyes, covered in a spray of thick white paint that had actually landed quite artistically.

Nothing but a ray of sunlight coming through the window.

Nothing.

Until the machines started, and the barricades began to come off.

CHAPTER TWELVE

In the lounge, there was a strange lack of bodies. No dead Deanna, Gugwana or Morwenna. Just their clothes lying crumpled on the floor where Daphne had seen her saviours fall, and Gugwana's beautiful decorative knife. Daphne picked that up and hid it in the kitchen. The whole house already felt different. It had lost the dark feeling that had crept in over the last few days and was starting to feel like home again. Warmer. The lovely old place where she grew up. That strange feeling of nostalgia for her mother, who she'd never known was a witch, though now so much was starting to make sense. The way she'd always managed to chase away her night terrors, which maybe were real after all.

The barricades were noisily removed from the front of the house, and Daphne opened the door to a beautiful sunny day on a green leafy street and a crowd of people, all looking at her. All seeing her. A couple of photographers, including one certain round-headed man who got his shot with a little knowing nod. Angela Shipman darted forward, sound recorder in hand. Daphne certainly wasn't invisible now. She didn't care.

And then, in the crowd of officers and civilians on all sorts of official business, she saw a face she was as happy as she was relieved to see. It was Sara, holding baby Alfie, both alive and well. Daphne ran straight over, brushing Shipman aside.

'I thought you were dead,' said Daphne.

'I knew you'd be alright,' replied Sara with a smile. 'But now we have much work to do, sister, and we cannot dally.' Sara turned and walked back into her house at number four, raised her hand, and the door flung itself shut.

***

Over the next few days and weeks as the summer diminished, so too did the police presence from Hanging Hill Lane. Occasionally a tourist would come by to see the site of the world-famous murders, now the six-eight-ten killings, as they had become known. Very rarely someone would come to knock on doors too, preaching the word of God, but they'd soon get chased away by Sara clutching an old broomstick.

Daphne forgave Olivia. People do strange things when they're that scared, but slowly they started to drift apart. Though they'd always be there for each other if needed, things were never quite the same after that, and Daphne didn't need a well-dressed, overly positive and outgoing role model anymore. She no longer wanted to be her, or anyone else she wasn't. Plus, she had her own teachers and guides at home now. As for Detective Inspector Bright, Daphne had soon after read in the news about a high-ranking police officer gone mad, claiming to have been possessed by the Devil himself and losing his job as a result. The employment tribunal hadn't gone well, and the process had uncovered all sorts of previous dodgy goings-on. That was the last she ever heard of him. Assuming it was him. Immoral. It must have been.

Neither head nor body of Andrew Foot was ever discovered, nor was anything in the news. Daphne desperately hoped that somehow, instead of simply vanishing the evidence, the witches had sent him back in time to when he was safe, and sometimes pictured him home with his family, slurping noodles in his weird way.

And Timothy? The beansprout man of God? She never saw him again. A few months later, on her nineteenth birthday, he'd sent her a friend request on social media, followed by a highly inappropriate photograph she really wished she'd never opened. She then spent three whole days reading up on memory-erasing witchcraft in the hopes that she could find some kind of spell to cast on herself that might just make it possible for her to somehow unsee. Beansprout indeed.

Anyway.

Daphne would babysit baby Alfie as he grew through the months. Now able to smile, he was playing on the lounge floor with a load of plastic toys and a big cuddly soft fox, making a mess all over the place. The doorbell chimed – the old ding dong had long gone, now replaced with something that sounded more like a heavy wind chime that was much more in keeping with the old house. Daphne checked the spyhole, but no one was there. When she opened the door, she looked around and saw no one. Nothing. Just an empty road lined with leafy green trees defying the months now well into autumn. No police, no press, and no red-haired Morwenna Rowe standing across the street. Instead, by her feet, was a hare. The hare hopped into the house past Daphne's feet, who smiled and laughed as she closed the door and saw the hare turn the corner and leap out of view into her lounge.

Walking back in, Daphne was greeted and thanked by Sara as she hugged Alfie on the floor, grabbing his little bag ready to leave. Sara often did that when she was in a rush. A hare can travel much faster than a human form, after all.

'Goodbye, ladies,' Sara said as she left. Daphne didn't mind being left to tidy up. It was an excuse to practice.

'Plastic, plastic, and you, little fox, get yourselves inside the box!' commanded Daphne to the mess on the floor, with a kind of awkward upward inflexion that kind of sounded like she was asking a question. The plastic toys jumped up and flew across the room, missing the box by a mile. The fox landed in front of the three mannequins, now wearing the clothes of Deanna Tamblyn, Morwenna Rowe, and Gugwana Imamu, as Daphne now knew her full name to be, dressed in her distinctive long, bright clothing, knife clipped onto her belt. Daphne stood tall and looked at the mannequins.

'I hope the war isn't coming too soon,' she said. 'I've got so much to learn.'

The room grew a little brighter as Gugwana's mannequin head turned to give Daphne the most beautiful smile a mannequin could ever smile.

But her greatest teacher was yet to come. She'd been putting it off every day, desperate to do it but fearing the pain it would bring would be too much. Finally, today was the day. She'd ordered a beautiful new mannequin and it had just arrived, and she'd stood it proudly next to Gugwana, one of her mother's best friends in this world.

She walked over and knelt by the box of her mother's things, stroking the top of it with her fingertips, feeling emotional but strong.

'Okay Mum,' she said, 'let's get you out of here.'

And opened the box.

Epilogue

And though she had escaped a fateful death,
Nature stepped inside and said: *Not yet...*

The three who fell still stood but now stood still,
Two demons down, a law swept in as well.

A law of nature older than the trees...
That demons move as witches do...

And always come
In threes.

To those who loved this book

Thank you so much for reading. If you liked this book, please consider giving a review at Amazon as that is a *huge* way other people will find it. Reviews are gold to authors, and I would be very grateful. Or feel free not to, of course. Either way, thank you for reading, and hopefully see you on the next one.

Phil

ABOUT THE AUTHOR

Philip Alexander Baker started his writing career as lyricist for indie band Lemanis, which released two albums, *Shell*, and *The Truth Behind the Push-Me-Pull-You*. Life as a filmmaker and screenwriter followed, including writing the award-winning *A Story for Happy*, and producing the British crime drama films *Killing Lionel* and *Card Dead*.

This is his first book.

Twitter.com/Phil_Baker_

Facebook.com/PhilipAlexanderBaker

Instagram.com/Phil_Baker_

9 781739 274108